D0036609

BEYOND THE DESERT GATE

ALSO BY MARY RAY

THE ROMAN EMPIRE SEQUENCE

A Tent for the Sun

The Ides of April

Sword Sleep

Beyond the Desert Gate

Rain from the West

BEYOND THE DESERT GATE

MARY RAY

BETHLEHEM BOOKS • IGNATIUS PRESS
Bathgate, N.D. San Francisco

This edition slightly revised by the author

Cover design by Davin Carlson

First Bethlehem Books printing, February 2001

ISBN 978-1-883937-54-6
Library of Congress catalog card number: 00-108547

Bethlehem Books • Ignatius Press
10194 Garfield Street South
Bathgate, ND 58216
www.bethlehembooks.com

Printed in the United States on acid free paper

CONTENTS

Mediterranean Sea
PHOENICIA
SYRIA
Damascus
Caesarea Philippi
GAULANITIS
GALILEE
Jotapata
Sea of Galilee
Tiberias
TRACHONITIS
DECAPOLIS
Caesarea
Scythopolis
Gerasa
SAMARIA
River Jordan
PERAEA
Gadora
Philadelphia
Jericho
Jerusalem
Dead Sea
Macherus
JUDAEA
N
NABATAEA
Eilat
Miles
0 10 20 30
0 20 40
Kilometres
Palestine AD 68-70

Author's Note

PALESTINE, for the people of the two generations before A.D. 69 when this book begins, had been a deeply divided and unhappy place in which to live. The strip of land three hundred miles long between Damascus in the north and Eilat in the south, and inland from the Mediterranean across to the high plateau of Jordan is only half the size of England, and yet after the death of King Herod the Great in 4 B.C. it was divided and subdivided a dozen times under kings, tetrarchs and Roman procurators who often ruled lands no bigger than an English county—Judaea, Galilee, Peraea, Trachonitis, Ituraea. Not one of the descendants of Herod approached him in political skill, and the procurators who succeeded him in Judaea were seldom better than the weak and stubborn Pontius Pilate, and often very corrupt.

After his recall the situation grew much worse, the country was torn by the conflicts between political and religious factions and by Zealot risings which were put down with great cruelty. At last the Emperor decided to end an intolerable situation and in A.D. 67 Palestine was invaded from the north by the legate of Syria, Vespasian, commanding the Xth, XIIth and XVth legions. The complete subjugation of the country took six years, from the first of several invasions to the capture of Masada in A.D. 73.

Ever since the death of Alexander, who had captured Palestine in 332 B.C. there had been Greek cities co-existing side by side with the Jewish population. They are mentioned in the New Testament as the Decapolis—the ten cities—and were governed mainly as the old cities of Greece had been by their own magistrates, but by now under the general eye of Rome. Much of this book takes place in the most southerly of them, Philadelphia, the modern Amman, capital of Jordan. It had once been Rabbath bene Ammon of the old Ammonite kingdom. The walls of the citadel still stand around the small central hill in the middle of the large modern Arab city, and the ruins of the Roman forum provide a convenient short cut across the centre from one bus station to another.

The very detailed knowledge we have of the Jewish war comes mostly from one source. Josephus was a Jew, onetime commander of the defenders of Jotapata in Galilee when it was besieged, who went over to Rome after its capture. He came into favour with Vespasian by interpreting a Jewish prophecy, that one who came from Judaea would rule the world, to mean that he would become Emperor; Christians, of course, interpret it differently. Vespasian did become Emperor in A.D. 69 and later Josephus was commissioned to write an official account of the campaign. It is he who tells us about Eleazer of Macherus, who suffered exactly as I have described.

PHILADELPHIA A.D. 69

DRAMATIS PERSONÆ

APOLLODORUS OF PHILADELPHIA	a Greek merchant
CONAN	his sons
NICANOR	
PHILOKLES	
LUCIA	his housekeeper
CHARES	a farmer, his cousin
PAULINUS	a banker of Philadelphia
TIMON OF GERASA	a merchant
GORION	a Jewish scribe
XENOS	the stranger
MARIUS GALLIENUS	tribune of the Xth Legion
DECIMUS	a centurion
FULVIUS	mess steward

BEYOND THE DESERT GATE

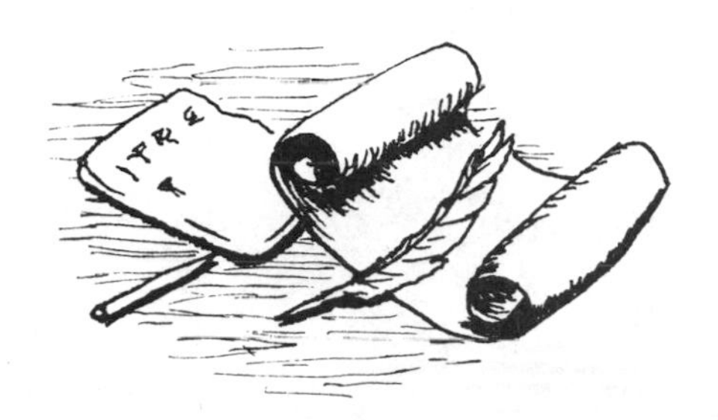

I

MEN FROM THE DESERT

THE CITADEL HILL of Philadelphia was cupped between the higher slopes on either side like the smallest egg in a basket, but from the bastion above the southern gate you could see a little way down the desert road, so Philo often came there in the afternoon when school was over and it was too hot to go to the gymnasium. Timas had always been with him till midsummer, before the fever; now Philo went alone. Philadelphia was a new city, even the walls were new, but there were plants growing in the cracks already, and the beginnings of lichen. Where they faced towards the desert to the south and east the stinging sand blown in by hot winds was already weathering the new stone.

Today there was no sand in the wind, only the choking dryness of the *hamsin,* as if the desert were breathing on the city. It was midsummer and the sky was like polished metal. All morning Philo had sweated in the airless schoolroom, and now, even on the walls which caught what breeze there was, his thinnest tunic was sticking to his back like a clammy second skin. He wished he had not come, but it was a habit to watch the last caravans of the day in through the gate below. His father, Apollodorus the merchant, was due home any day up the desert road that led south all the way to Eilat and the trade routes beyond.

The last donkeys, only feet and ears under their shapeless loads, were below him, and the builders' racket from the unfinished temple behind on the citadel hill had stilled for the day. It was time to go home. Philo slipped down from his perch on the wall and threaded his way through the steep streets and across the small square with the Council House and the temple of Zeus, down to the eastern side of the hill and home.

Most of the oldest houses were here. Fifty years before there had been only a herdsmen's village; now the marketplace and the new houses of merchants and tradesmen had spread into the narrow valley beyond the walls and the high hill beyond. It looked Greek, till you remembered the desert to the east and the great valley of the salt sea to the west and noticed the darker skins and eyes on the school benches along with the fairer hair of some of the merchants' sons.

Another day was over and his father had not come, but it was too soon to worry. In one way, with war so close across the river, times had never been so dangerous, but at least the Roman patrols on the roads had driven the robbers deeper into the desert. His friend Timas had died since Philo's father had gone south in spring; he was not ready yet to imagine more bad news. Suddenly he wanted his father back so much that he stopped in his tracks, one hand on the stone of a house wall that still gave out heat like a baking bread-oven. His brothers had said and done what they could, but Conan was eighteen and Nicanor seventeen; they had little time to spare for a schoolboy.

Half-way down the hill there were more people about, and a clatter of donkeys and cheerful shouting, the house gate was round the next corner; and then Philo began to run because he had recognized one of the voices, and it was not possible. How could Esdras his father's steward be cursing a mule-boy at the gate when he was still far down the desert road with Apollodorus?

Esdras was not. He was driving the beasts round to the back gate and the storeyard behind the house; neighbours had come to their doors to stare and chatter and the house sounded like a kicked bees' nest. Always Philo's heart seemed to stand still at this moment, waiting actually to hear his father's voice, to be really sure. Now, after so many afternoons of watching, he had managed to miss the caravan.

Philo nearly knocked over the old porter, beginning to swing the gate shut, as he ran through into the courtyard. From behind, like the actors on the stage in the new theatre, he saw his family. A tall man, still cloaked and hooded from the dust of the road, fair slim Conan and dark Nicanor, and old Lucia who had come with his mother when she married, lumbering from the kitchen with the master's use-polished silver cup full of cooled wine. No mother; that death was far back in his childhood.

Apollodorus took the cup and drained it, then he noticed his youngest son. Philo bent to kiss his father's hand, and then the dusty cloak with the smell of the desert and camels and safety was about him for a moment.

Apollodorus turned back towards the gate.

"Esdras! But I told him . . . never mind. Lucia, there's a sick man. I told Esdras to bring the mule this way, but he's taken him round to the storeyard with the others. We need somewhere cool and quiet."

"What sort of a man?" asked the housekeeper.

"I don't know, he was too ill to ask. Is there a bed in the

spare room next to Philo?" He turned towards the doors on the east side of the courtyard.

"Yes, but there's no bedding." Lucia, willing, but large and slow-moving on her bad legs, waddled off, calling the porter to help with a mattress.

Leading his sons like a small caravan Apollodorus strode through the arch that divided the courtyard containing the family's living quarters from the storeyard with its stables, kitchen and workrooms. The eastern side of the citadel hill was steep here and the yard was several steps up, with a gate into it at the back where a higher loop of the road ran behind the back wall. That gate was open now, three dust-coated donkeys stood with drooping heads and Esdras was leading in a curiously loaded mule.

The sick man was slung awkwardly and insecurely across a pannier, weighed down on the other side by a heavy sack; he seemed unconscious, his head flopping over the beast's rump, so shrouded from the sun that he looked like an untidy roll of carpet.

"Nico, help me, take his legs," said the merchant, going to support the head and shoulders, while Esdras held the mule still. "Philo, undo the ropes. We had to tie him on down in the market when we paid off the camel men. Careful, though, the sun's half flayed him."

The ropes were newly tied and the knots came undone easily. As Nicanor and his father lowered the man to the ground, the cloak that covered him fell back and showed his face. Philo, feeling his mouth go dry, blinked, but found he could not look away after all. He had never seen anyone in quite that state before, except the leprous beggar on the steps of the temple of Zeus, and as he had been growing slowly more repulsive for as long as anyone could remember there had been a chance to get used to him.

It was a moment before Philo recognized that he was looking at the worst sunburn he had ever seen, an oozing mass of blisters, paper-white in the middle, crusted and dark red where they joined. The man's eyelids were stuck shut, swollen and raw, and his cracked lips were half open. Only by the colour of the dark hair and beard, caked with sand and dirt, was it possible to guess his age.

Lucia called from the arch that they were ready. Apollodorus and Nicanor carried the man through.

Inside the small room Apollodorus dropped his heavy cloak and bent over the shape on the bed, unwrapping the coverings.

"We found him two evenings ago, just north of Macherus, pegged out in the sand where a Roman patrol had left him. I'm not sure we were kind to bring him back, it wouldn't have taken much longer and he was already unconscious."

Uncovered, the man was young and slimly built, all the upper surfaces of his body as flayed as his face, his wrists and ankles deeply scored with rope marks. The blisters had broken where the ties had supported him on camel and mule, cutting across the burned areas; the oozing places were festering already.

"My infusion of rue and rosemary is the only thing I can think of for those wounds," said Lucia, her lined old face puckered with concern. "His skin's in a terrible state but we must get him clean." Then she turned back to Apollodorus, clearly distracted with what to do first, dinner half cooked and now this new problem.

"Philo can help you, the boys can stow the goods away for the night, and I can take care of myself," said the merchant.

When the others had gone Lucia looked across at the boy doubtfully. "Just hold the bowl steady." She bathed the head and neck first, leaving the burnt areas till last, while Philo changed the water again and again till the last of the grit and dirt had gone; only then did she begin on the wounds about the man's eyes, with the thin green liquid that smelled of all the grazed knees Philo had ever had.

As the cool cloth touched his swollen eyelids the man moved and groaned for the first time; a tongue like leather flopped between his cracked lips.

"Lift his head." Lucia poured first a few drops and then a small trickle of water into the man's mouth and waited till she saw him swallow before pouring again. The sticky eyelids fluttered but stayed closed while the mouth moved again.

"He's trying to say something, can you hear?" Lucia asked.

Philo put his ear close to the man's mouth. "He says he's blind, I think."

Lucia smoothed the wet dark hair back gently and took the man's hand; there was an answering pressure. "No, poor soul, you're not blind. You just can't see through your eyelids. You'll have to be patient. Now lie quiet while we make you comfortable."

The head on the mattress turned slowly towards where her voice had been and then did not move again.

The kitchen-maid came to the doorway and stood nervously looking into the room. Lucia saw her shadow on the wall and partly covered the man on the bed before she turned.

"Not the soup again?"

"No, it's the sauce for the chickens."

"I'll come. Philo, you stay, he might speak again."

Without waiting for an answer she hurried out, leaving Philo alone. Flies were gathering at the unwashed sores on the man's shoulders and chest. He brushed them away and then sat down on a stool where the glare from the late afternoon sky, partly veiled by the thin cloud of the *hamsin,* lit the dusty little room. It was very hot.

The man on the bed made a noise in his throat and moved his head. Philo got up and looked down at him. He seemed to be thirsty again. It was awkward lifting the head and holding a cup at the same time, but he managed it without spilling much water down the man's neck. When he had had enough the sick man turned his head against Philo's shoulder and shut his mouth for the first time; it made him look quite different. Suddenly he was almost a person and clearly very tired; it was a shame he had to be kept waiting for the cleaning of his wounds before he could rest in comfort.

Philo was fourteen and reasonably good with his hands if he was interested in what he was doing, but this was the most difficult thing he had ever attempted. He turned back the covers and picked up the sponge and the bowl of lotion. Working a small area at a time he did what he could. The body smelled of sweat and blood and dirt, and he broke some of the blisters he was trying to clean, but all the time he was working the man did not cry out or move again.

He must have a name but he can't tell us, Philo thought, as he worked. He looks Greek like us, I'm sure that beard and the shape of his head are Greek, not Syrian or any other mixture. I shall call him Xenos, because he's a guest and a stranger. I wonder what he'd done to make the patrol treat him like that?

He picked up the right arm and began to bathe the rope sores around the wrist. The fingers were long and the hand well-shaped, and as he turned it over he noticed a characteristic bump on the middle finger. Xenos was used to holding a pen.

Philo was so intent on what he was doing that he did not hear his father outside and only looked up when the light from the doorway was blocked out. Apollodorus had been standing watching his third son with surprise and approval; he would have expected Philo to be too sensitive for such an unpleasant job. All he said was, "You've finished? Good, Atius will sit with him now while we eat."

The lamps had been lit in the dining-room with its terra-cotta-coloured walls by the time the family had finished eating, and Lucia was letting in a small stream of friends and business associates to share the wine and news of the newly returned merchant.

Apollodorus's face was grave; there was no need to tell anyone what was happening in the tormented land of Judaea across the river, where only the death of the Emperor Nero the year before had halted the long war to subdue the Jewish people. Since then there had been two Emperors, and old Vespasian, legate of Syria, had waited and drawn back his legions from Jerusalem until he was sent new authority. But the war was not over, Roman auxiliaries still patrolled the desert, blockading those isolated Jewish forts which continued to hold out.

"The roads are full again of hopeless bands of refugees with their sick babies and overloaded beasts," said the merchant.

"But you got through?" questioned Paulinus, a banker. "You made your usual profit?"

"Yes, we got through, but for the profit—I don't know. Who wants to buy pearls when a province is collapsing?"

"Rome, my friend, always Rome. The ladies there would buy even though a province was lost every morning before they opened their eyes and called for breakfast. But you'll have to trade again further north up towards Syria to get a good price."

"There was talk that you brought in a wounded man," said Timon of Gerasa. "If the roads were as bad as you say, why one out of so many?"

Philo had been wondering that, but had been afraid to ask before his father's guests.

"A good question," said Apollodorus, shifting his long body on the cushions as if he was still unaccustomed to comfort, and smiling to himself. "I suppose it was just because he was one alone, and once I lived somehow alone myself for three days when I was a young man, and a bad caravan leader left me behind."

There was more to it than that and Philo nearly asked about the Roman patrol who had staked Xenos out; then he saw how his father was looking at Paulinus the banker. He was the most powerful man in Philadelphia, but among the other merchants in the room there was no one who liked or fully trusted him. One did not give into his hands anything that could bring danger or give excuse for harm.

Soon Paulinus excused himself and left and most of the others went not long after. When only Timon of Gerasa, the family's oldest friend, was left, they spoke of Xenos again.

"Is there any talk in the market of how we found him?" asked Apollodorus.

"Not much. The drivers you were with don't belong here, they'll be on their way in the morning. I did hear you'd rescued him from the Romans, but it seemed such an unlikely tale that the man who was spreading it was laughed at and went off in a huff. It isn't true, is it?"

"Not quite like that. We didn't have a pitched battle with a patrol. I suppose it was a stupid thing to do, and I was telling myself that even while we were packing the poor man on to a baggage camel."

"We have to live alongside Rome," said Timon. "Why ask for trouble?"

"Yes, as we live in the desert with snakes and scorpions. If I give the viper time to slide away, and keep my hand from the scorpion beneath the stone, it will not sting me. We share the same ground but we still fear and hurt each other."

"We're right on the edge here," said Timon. "I wonder that we small cities survive at all. We're like the flower that grows in the crack in a wall, clinging on till one day added to another makes up our lifetime. Things come to us—from Rome or the desert—and we can do little about it."

"Father, tell us where you found the man—Xenos or whatever his name really is," said Conan.

"It was before the *hamsin* started and we'd been making good time. I knew we couldn't reach here by nightfall and would have to camp somewhere, though the caravan leader would have liked to push on. I spoke against that as my mule was lame. It was then that we saw a dust cloud ahead on the road. From the hoof marks it seemed to be a Roman patrol ahead of us, mounted auxiliaries, possibly Arabians—that pegging out is one of their tricks. It was some time later, where the road forks to the pass above Macherus, that we found him. I have a feeling that our Xenos could have come from the fortress there and been overtaken by the patrol."

"There's nothing on the east side of the lake below Macherus but burned villages and ruined water holes, from what I've heard," said Timon. "A cruel business. Why did Vespasian have to send his bullies across Jordan? He has trouble stored up in Judaea and the people of Peraea were quiet enough, they were too poor to be anything else."

"A military man would say that he had to secure his flank, and there to the east is Macherus sticking up like a thorn, still garrisoned from Jerusalem. Perhaps Xenos is a Jewish spy turned awkward."

"No, he's not a Jew," said Philo, and then stopped, blushing at the sound of his own voice.

"How do you know?" asked his father with a smile. "Oh, I forgot, you helped wash him. What do you think he is? A farmer, a soldier?"

"Neither of those, he has good hands and he's used to writing; I think he's Greek."

"Then he'll be all the more interesting to talk to when he comes round, if he does. Do you think he can live?" Apollodorus turned to Lucia, standing behind him holding a wine jug.

"I don't know, he may not. He has fever, and his body's so dry—sometimes they don't recover, men brought in from the desert like that."

That was when Philo was sent to bed. He went first to the doorway of the sick man's room next to his own, but all was dark and quiet except for the snores of old Atius the porter, who was supposed to be keeping an eye on Xenos. He was afraid to go in.

Lying without a cover on his own bed he could see the lights and hear voices from the other side of the courtyard. Conan and Nicanor passed the doorway, arguing together as usual; their room was beyond his. Now Philo had time to be puzzled by what his father had done; he knew Apollodorus to be wise and just but he was not often impulsive, those narrow 'desert' eyes had seen too much. As Timon had said, why this one man out of all the suffering men he had seen? Perhaps some God was in it. From what Philo had heard as his brothers passed, Nicanor was angry as well as puzzled; that was nothing new. His dark shy brother, very like their dead half-Jewish mother, had never found life easy and was usually suspicious of anything new, and who could tell what upsets a very sick enemy of Rome would cause in the household? Conan was tall and good-looking, with the confidence that good looks often bring, and the unconcern over other people's problems; he was far more interested in the details of his father's journey than the future of a sick man he had so far hardly seen.

Philo rolled over to let the air get to his damp skin, wondering why it was that Xenos interested him so much that he wished he was next door on the mattress, not Atius, except that if the stranger had woken he would not have known what to do. If Xenos did die without speaking they would never know who he was, and he could not bear the thought of that. When he slept at last his dreams were frightening and confused.

II

A COHORT OF THE X^{TH}

PHILO WOKE early and lay listening to the sounds of the house. It always felt different when his father was at home and there were a man's footsteps and voice about. He thought Lucia had gone in to the sick man next door very early; Philo wanted an excuse to go himself but was suddenly uncharacteristically shy. It was going to be another burning day and he was thirsty, that gave him an idea. He dressed quickly and went to the well to draw a jug of cold water.

From the doorway Xenos looked rather better, as if the face under the blisters was firmer and the lips less cracked; Philo went across and touched one of the hands that lay limp, palm down on the mattress. It was still hot with fever, but the fingers moved and clasped his.

"Are you thirsty?" Philo bent close and spoke quietly. The dark head turned on the pillow, trying to follow the voice, and the lips parted.

He raised Xenos's head as he had done the evening before and tilted the cup. The man drank more easily this time. When Philo had rested his head back the fingers of his hand moved again, as if searching for something and Philo took the hand in both of his.

"I can still hear horses, but I'm on a bed, I think." The

voice was as light as the wind in dry leaves and the stiff lips stumbled over the words, but the meaning was quite clear.

"You can hear donkeys in the road. It's steep outside the house and they always clatter keeping their feet on the corner."

"Whose house?"

"Ours, my father's. Apollodorus of Philadelphia, he found you."

"Where was I?"

"Don't you remember? On the road above Macherus where the Romans left you."

The head on the pillow turned away as if in disbelief, but then shifted back as if Xenos was still trying to see through his swollen eyelids. "I don't remember Macherus or anything. Who am I?"

"We don't know, we thought you would tell us. I called you Xenos last night because you were a stranger; you must be Greek because that's what we're speaking."

"Xenos! Well, a name is a beginning. It's been dark and empty alone inside my head."

His fingers slipped free.

"School!" said Conan from the doorway. "Father says sick strangers are no excuse. Hurry up, you aren't too old to be beaten."

Philo gave Xenos a last anxious look, but the man seemed to need nothing more than to be left in quiet to rest. He was still an ugly sight, but there had been something about his voice and the few words he had said. Not, "Where am I?" like people were supposed to say. It was going to be very hard to concentrate on Aristotle.

Apollodorus went out later, taking Conan with him. The eldest son of the house was studying law with the only teacher the city could provide, but his father was anxious that he should learn as much as he could about his own business and took him on the usual round of visits to bankers and clients that followed every journey. Dark, quiet Nicanor had gone back to his favourite place, the farm of his father's cousin up the northern Gerasa road. Nicanor loved animals and spent as much time as he could outside the noisy high-walled city.

The market-place stood on the level ground below the east side of the citadel hill. It was late morning when Apollodorus and his eldest son passed through it for the second time, and at once the merchant sensed that something was disturbing the usual gossip and selling. Some stall-holders seemed to be packing up already, and women were hurrying away with their loaded baskets, but knots of young men were gathering and buzzing like bees in thundery weather wondering whether to swarm.

Apollodorus caught at the arm of a councillor hurrying past. "What is it? What's going on?"

"Trajan, legate of the tenth legion, that's who, and a cohort of his men and more auxiliaries than I care to see near a partially walled city. Excuse me, we have to arrange a deputation to receive him."

"Are we going to be attacked?" Conan felt his heart start to thud with an excitement that was only partly frightening.

"No, I don't think it's danger we should be worried about so much as nuisance. That is, if everyone keeps his head and no one annoys a drunken centurion and starts a fight. We're used to Romans in the city, but a few at a time, not a whole cohort. We're still allies of Rome, even if we don't like them. It's the Jews we have reason to fear, particularly since the attack three years ago."

Conan remembered only too well, although he had heard more than he had actually seen. He had been fifteen when the raiding parties from Galilee, wrought up almost to insanity by suffering and religious intolerance, had crossed the Jordan and gone on a Greek hunt through the ten cities. Up on the citadel hill in a house with strong walls the family had been safe enough, but he would not be likely to forget his first smell of violence, the smoke drifting from the rows of mean shacks behind the market, the colour and choking stench when whole houses and their contents went up, and the noise men make when they are hunting to kill and when they die. And it had been dry for many days after the attackers had been driven off; it had taken a long time for the marks of blood to be washed from the streets.

It had made it no easier that his mother had Jewish blood, but they had always known it was safer not to discuss that outside the family.

"Look, they're here!" His father pulled him back into the arched entry of a grain warehouse as the first horsemen cantered into a suddenly silent square.

A young tribune in a flaunting scarlet cloak, dark-skinned and dark-haired, paced his mount out into the clear space in the centre; a jerk of his head distributed his men round the edge, covering the main roads that led down from the citadel hill and north and south up the narrow valley between the high ground on either side. It was suddenly even quieter except for a few curt orders, and the sound of hooves grating on the cobbles as the horses fidgeted. Conan heard the hens in a basket that had been hastily pushed under a half-clear stall begin to cluck and protest.

Then he heard another sound, regular and deep, like the pulse of a distant drum, one he had never heard before but which caught at his belly and made him gasp—the mailed sandals of a cohort on the march.

The tribune called his guard to attention, for the legate himself rode at the head of his men, the Trajan who the year before had besieged Jotapata in Galilee for forty-seven days and watched while the few of her people who still survived were driven down over the steep cliffs of their city. He was thin and grey-haired, his great white cloak spreading over the rump of a black horse, but he had the dangerousness of a grey sword blade. Behind him the first two centuries of his men followed him into the square and crashed to a halt.

A small and rather raggedly arranged group of city elders were hurrying down from the temple of Zeus on the hill. The legate awaited their arrival with no show of impatience, while the crowd that was spilling from the side streets muttered and stared.

"Why are they here?" whispered Conan.

"They must have come down the north road to link up with the desert patrols. If the magistrates make the right speeches they'll probably do no more harm than take a week's rations as a gift. But those are the men who sacked Gadora last year and they may be getting bored. I'm not sure they can really tell the difference between a friendly city that just wants to keep out of trouble and a Jewish garrsion learning to fear life more than death. Come on, let's fetch your brother home from school before the centurions let that lot out to look for amusement."

The school was round on the west side of the citadel hill, and they reached it by way of the side door of the warehouse and back streets almost before news of the arrival of the legion had spread so far. The schoolmaster took one look at Apollodorus's face and closed his tablets with a snap. Conan noticed with amusement that Philo seemed to be the next but one to recite and that his relief at the diversion was comic. What with his father's return and the arrival of Xenos he had clearly not done his homework.

"Can't we go down just for a little while to see what's happening?" he asked as his father led the way home.

"You don't know what you're talking about, don't be a fool," snapped Apollodorus. "Now, keep close."

They were at the end of their own street when a mounted patrol clattered past. The sudden smell of dust thrown up and sweating horses seemed to Philo as he pressed back against a wall to be the very scent of danger itself. After he had seen the faces of the men he knew why his father had hurried. The patrol went by without stopping. Their porter dropped the beam that secured the house gate behind them with a comforting crash; Lucia was waiting for them in the courtyard.

"We're here, all safe," said Apollodorus. "Except Nicanor, and he'll have the sense to stay where he is." He turned back to the porter. "No one opens that gate for any reason except by my orders and in my presence."

Then there was a feeling of anticlimax. The city outside was only a little quieter than usual at the hour after noon on a warm day. Lucia stumped off towards the kitchen, murmuring about an early lunch, while Apollodorus went through to the storeyard shouting for Esdras as if nothing had happened.

Philo went quietly into Xenos's room and stood by the bed. The sick man sensed at once that he was not alone. "Who is it? Is it you?" He did not know Philo's name.

"I'm Philo, but you won't know who we are till you can see us."

Then he was horrified because Xenos was trying to cry, the tears oozing stickily from his swollen eyelids. Lucia had left a bowl and a cloth by the bed. Philo bathed them very gently with clean water and the right eye opened just a crack. Xenos caught his breath.

"There is light, it's still there."

"Of course it is, it's nearly midday. Go to sleep again and when you wake the other one will probably open."

Xenos gave the ghost of a smile at the mixture of nervousness and authority in the boy's voice and managed to turn partly over on his side. Quite soon his breathing settled to the steady rhythm of sleep. Philo stood a little longer watching him, then he bent closer. The thin cover had fallen away from the curve of Xenos's spine and his shoulders were bare. Regularly across them was the white grid of scars left from an old beating, something far worse than Philo had ever endured or known his father to order for anyone in the household. Somehow it did not fit with the quiet voice and the clever hands. That would be something else to ask Xenos when he could speak.

But the rest of the day dragged on quietly in the merchant's house. Xenos slept till nearly evening and only woke long enough to be fed a bowl of bread sops in broth and then went to sleep again. Lucia, looking down at him, allowed herself to be hopeful and would not disturb him even to dress his burns.

And the city outside was quiet although more than once marching feet passed the house; then after sunset there was shouting and the light of a fire from near the market-place.

Apollodorus went up on to the roof to look down between the lower buildings and came down saying grimly that even in so small a city the men had found some amusement. Conan took turns with his father and Esdras after that to keep watch through the night, but it passed quietly.

In the small room off the storeyard the man Xenos woke with the first cock and lay in the now familiar darkness nursing a raw arm where the blisters had broken as he stretched. The garment of pain that seemed to have covered him for longer than he could remember had settled everywhere else to the quiet discomfort of a scratchy blanket, except in the places that had started to itch. He knew that was probably a good thing, but it promised to be a bother later.

Very gently he put a hand up to his face and felt the sticky crust over his eyes and the unfamiliar papery stiffness of cheeks and forehead. He knew he had been burned by the sun; had the young voice who came and went told him or did he remember? What sun could have done this and in what land? How long had it taken? How long to cure a goat-hide sewn tight across its frame?

He had been tied, ropes had pulled him taut across the rocky ground, he remembered the jagged edges under his shoulders that after a while he had no longer noticed because by then the sun was high. Then the painfully echoing loneliness inside his head was split and shattered with the full memory of that sun and of what had come before, so that he whimpered and clasped at the edge of the mattress where he lay, to make sure that it was really over and only weakness was holding him still. Atius on the floor grunted and turned but did not wake, and after a while the man too lay quietly, waiting for the dawn he could not see and the hands from nowhere that tended him and might help him to live with this other now-remembered pain.

Philo came to the door of his father's bedroom early. Apollodorus, who had taken the middle watch in the night, was only just waking, but he sat up quickly and reached for his sandals when he heard what his son had to say.

"Xenos has remembered; not everything, but why he was in the desert. He seems much better and the fever's gone. I think he wants to talk."

They went together into the room. Xenos's head turned on the pillow when he heard their voices and footsteps.

"I am Apollodorus who found you," said the merchant. "My son says you would like to talk to us. Would you rather have your wounds dressed first?"

"No, please, that will hurt and I want to be able to think clearly. It's inside me now, I'm . . . shut in with it because it's the only thing I can remember. I don't know why I did what I did. I can't go back to anything before the road up from the salt sea. But you, sir, must sometimes do illogical things, or I wouldn't be here. I've caused you a good deal of trouble, and it's not really a healthy activity for a merchant to rescue a man whom the Romans have condemned to die."

"Each man's conscience is his own, as I think you understand very well," said Apollodorus, smiling. Although the man in the bed could not see the smile, it showed in the voice, and Xenos smiled back.

"How long ago was it?"

"You have been here two nights—in Philadelphia of the ten cities—and we found you two evenings before that."

"Where did you come from?" asked Philo.

"I think I know the name but I can't remember why I was there or what it was like. Would it be Jerusalem?"

"You have travelled a difficult journey then, friend. What were you doing there?"

"I don't know, that's what's so uncanny. Yesterday I couldn't remember anything—who I was, what language I was speaking. Today it's like breaks in the cloud. I can remember places, Rome, Athens I think. I'm sure I've been there, but what I was doing in Jerusalem and why I was trying to get away with a party of women and children and wounded men I don't know. We were making for Macherus."

"Vespasian still has patrols out between Jericho and the cities up here on the plateau. He doesn't want anyone to escape from what will happen to Jerusalem."

"I think we knew that, but all I really remember is night and difficult roads, not fighting. Exhausted children, a beast going lame, you know. The moment comes when you think it would be easier to die where you are rather than struggle further on. I suppose that must have been what happened five nights ago, otherwise I don't know why I did it. I don't think I knew the people very well, I had no kin among them."

"And you don't know your name?" asked Philo, but when he saw that that distressed Xenos, he put his own hand over the fingers that had clenched again on the edge of the mattress.

Xenos's fingers loosened and clasped him back, and did not let go when he spoke again.

"No, that's what hurts worst. Not to have a name. We came to the ascent to Macherus at the beginning of the night. I think we must have been hiding by day. You know the heat of the Jordan valley, even if it hadn't been crawling with Vespasian's men. I think we knew that we would be safe in Macherus if we could reach it. But then we found that we had a patrol behind us. They must have cleared the road once already because we found the bodies, we knew what would happen if they caught up with us. The mounted auxiliaries had stopped asking who people were before they killed them and they seemed to prefer killing women to men."

He was silent for a moment, but the thin fingers still gripped Philo very tightly. When he spoke again his voice had gone flat, as if he was finding it difficult to control.

"I remember the leader of our group, his name was Jochanon, a big man with a huge beard and his right arm in a sling. Our group was quite large, in the pass it would have been difficult to hide. The patrol was coming up fast and there was no chance that we could escape unless we had more time."

He stopped again, and then said in a stronger voice, "I can't think why I imagined it would work! Why in heaven did I do it? I'm not a soldier—no, that at least I do know. It wasn't my sort of an idea."

"What did you do, friend?" asked Apollodorus.

"I asked Jochanon what the patrol would do if they thought they had stumbled on a large encampment. He said they would stop to reconnoitre it carefully before they attacked. For all they knew it might be Nabateans from Petra or merchants like you, and the Romans have no quarrel with them at the moment. He asked me what was in my mind. I said fires, four or five of them, and the two noisiest donkeys, one of which was lame and no loss to anyone. I thought that if I could delay the patrol an hour it might be long enough. He didn't think it was likely that I could but he agreed that it was worth trying, if that was what I wanted to do. It did work; it was nearer two hours before they finally rode in between the fires and found me alone prodding the donkey."

"Two hours!" whispered Apollodorus.

"Yes, a little after midnight, and it was—an hour after dawn, the sun was up—when they tied me out."

"Why didn't they kill you outright?"

"They seemed to think that because I had caused them so much trouble I must be trying to protect someone important, but I wasn't. Except isn't everyone important to themselves? But they . . ."

His hands broke free from Philo. It was all there now, passing behind his swollen eyelids, the hot night wind and flaring torches, the humiliation of complete helplessness, the harsh Roman voices and, at the end, pain. And behind the pain a deeper horror that this had all happened before and perhaps in spite of what was being done to him, things which must end soon, in a few hours he would wake up as one does after some dreams that keep returning, and it would all be to suffer again.

"He said—the centurion—as they were tying me out, 'Tell the sun, then, whatever it is you know, if he'll listen. We'll catch up with your friends soon enough without your help. Or you could tell the first hyena to find you tonight, if you're still alive. But I doubt if you'll last so long, a pity because they like their meat fresh.' Then they all laughed, particularly the man whose idea it had been, and wheeled their horses almost on top of me so that I thought I was going to be trampled, but all I got was a mouthful of dust."

He was crying with deep sobs that shook his whole body. Apollodorus slipped an arm round him to hold him steady against his shoulder.

"And are you sorry? You know that what you did was an

act that the Gods should reward and for which men should praise you."

Xenos steadied himself with a hand on the merchant's arm. "I know, but when I'm still in pain and the hours go on and on, I have to live or try to live with the results of what I did. It seems that honour is going to last a great deal longer than I had planned for." His voice caught again in what was almost a laugh. "And what God will reward me when I cannot even remember who it is that I have worshipped?"

III

THE HORSES OF CHARES

"THAT MAKES Xenos a hero, like Horatius holding the bridge against the enemies of Rome, doesn't it, Conan?" said Philo. "Have you ever met anyone who's done anything as brave as that?"

"Father told us about a camel driver who left a caravan far out in the desert and went back alone to try to find a cousin who had been lost in the night. He did too, and brought him back, though no one else would go with him and the leader wouldn't wait."

"Yes, but that man didn't know for sure he would be killed; he only took a risk that he might die himself," objected Philo.

"Xenos didn't die either; Father found him." Conan was being logical. Philo felt his face flush and tried not to get cross; he knew by now that that only made his older brother more irritating.

They were sitting on sacks in the warehouse on the far side of the storeyard, a dusty, sunny place that smelt more pungent than a scent shop, because most of Apollodorus's business was in spices, and the results of his last trip were stored here. He left the larger and more exotic goods, bales of silk, ivory and rare animals, to merchants with more capital who could afford the porters and camel men to protect them, and preferred himself to deal only in smaller articles of high value, spices, pearls and precious stones. Apart from the spices they were mostly things he could carry on his body, as he travelled with only Esdras for company.

At the third hour he had ordered the great beam to be drawn back from the door and had gone down into the city alone. All seemed quiet and his business would not stand more delay. Conan had instructions to sort and list packages of cinnamon, cloves and pepper. As an experienced elder brother he knew now that trouble might be coming and changed the subject.

"Philo, stop sitting on sacks I haven't checked! We shall all know more when Xenos remembers who he is. Until then there isn't much point discussing it. Do you know Father's planning to go north? Well, he said he might take me!"

"Why? You're going to be a lawyer. He promised to take me one day because I'm quite good at picking up languages and that's useful. More than law would be in the desert."

"Well, he hasn't exactly said, but it's as if these last two days he suddenly wanted me to know as much about the business as possible."

"You mean so that you could run it if he got killed? But you're much too young, it'd be years before you could manage alone."

Philo had said exactly what Conan thought was in his father's mind but neither of them had put into words. The very idea of it was frightening Conan so much that he couldn't control his face and turned his back to his brother, fussing over the ropes around the last sack till he felt a little better.

"Philo, honestly!"

"But what would we do?" asked Philo. "We're old enough to have to think about things like that. All around us for years cities have been going up in flames and people dying. Just because at the moment most of it has happened on the other side of the Jordan doesn't mean it couldn't happen here; all these little tetrarchies and independent cities are so small. All rolled together they hardly make one decent province. I'm not surprised that Nero lost patience with the Jews. I've been thinking, and I've no idea how I could earn my own living if Father suddenly didn't come back. Though I suppose he's as likely to come back and find no Philadelphia!"

There was a noise of sandals clattering in the other courtyard as the porter opened the gate.

"Father!" said Conan, dropping what he was doing and going to the doorway, grateful for the interruption.

"Do you think you really won't be a lawyer now?" Philo asked as he followed him. "Do you mind?"

"I think I did at first, but I've seen this coming for some time, and I would have needed better teaching than I could get here. Father couldn't afford to send me to Caesarea even if it was safe to go—which it isn't. It's better to be realistic, and it would be good to work for Father."

Philo suddenly hated Conan for making him bring out into the open something he would rather not have talked about; he even hated Conan for being old enough to be some practical help to his father and to have a chance of going on a journey. He had always dreamed about the morning when he would first ride out at dawn, down the valley that led to the desert gate and the whole world that lay beyond it.

Apollodorus seemed in a good humour again, he shouted for Esdras and then crossed over to the warehouse.

"Nearly done? Yes, the Romans are going. The word is that they're leaving half a century and some sick and wounded to form a depot and collect stores for patrols controlling the roads north and south of here. They've made a camp north of the city where the valley widens. There doesn't seem to be too much damage—a row of wine shops in the lower town burned out last night and some other small bits of trouble when the nearer farms lost livestock."

"Not Cousin Chares's farm?" asked Conan.

"I hadn't thought of that. It's to the north too. Perhaps you should take the mule and ride that way later. We leave the day after tomorrow with Timon. It should be safe to go north by then if we make up a party to travel with. Better tell Lucia now."

Conan went in the direction of the kitchen, looking preoccupied. "School for you tomorrow," said Apollodorus to his youngest son. "Come and show me how far you've got with the spices. They'll need repacking for Gerasa."

For the rest of the afternoon Philo tried to keep his mind on the packing and not on the disturbing topic of his talk with Conan. And he tried to keep away from Xenos, although the sick man drew his thoughts like a lodestone. From the first moment that he had seen him something had attracted him, repulsive as Xenos had looked. Now he could not quite come to terms with the unexpected horror of Xenos's story, or with the unexpected way he seemed to feel about it himself. Heroes were supposed to enjoy being heroic. Herakles could not have gone about with a self-satisfied grin on his face for months after every successful labour, but it had never occurred to Philo that coping with the consequences of heroism, living with the results to oneself, might be difficult and painful.

Philo knew that while they had been working in the warehouse Lucia had dressed Xenos's burns and bathed his eyes, because when he had looked in the man had been resting, clearly very tired. It was late afternoon before he found him awake again.

Xenos was trying to loosen the bandage Lucia had left over his eyes. It had dried and stiffened and looked very uncomfortable.

"Shall I take it off?" Philo asked. "Steady, it's stuck." He loosened it with the sponge the housekeeper had left.

"Philo? Yes, I know your voice and your touch now," said Xenos. "Have you ever nursed anyone before? You seem quite good at it."

"I don't know about that! Actually, I'm learning on you. Sorry, I shall have to pull the last bit."

Xenos winced but kept his head still. Philo stood back and looked at him. "You look so much better now I think I could have recognized you!"

"If you'd known what I looked like—which I don't myself!" Xenos raised his hands very gently to his eyes. "Your servant was right, the swelling's nearly down. Do you think you could bathe them again? Has she left the lotion here?"

"Yes, but do you really want me to do it? Shall I call her?"

"What time is it? No, I think I can feel because the sun's on the bed. Late afternoon, she'll be busy with the meal. I trust you, Philo, though it's hardly fair to expect you to look after me like this. Haven't you a friend waiting for you to go out? I know you've been working most of the day."

Something about the silence that followed pierced through Xenos's darkness as clearly as his sight could have.

"There isn't a friend?" he asked in a different voice.

"There was, till summer. Timas . . . He died of the wasting fever."

There was nothing to be said to that, and Xenos guessed more than Philo could have told him. He heard a clinking as the bowl of lotion was picked up and then felt the mixed sensation of cold and pain as the sponge touched his skin.

The eyelids were certainly much better, hardly more swollen than with a fever, and the crusts round the lashes had almost gone. With all the care that his fingers were capable of Philo bathed them away, while Xenos lay uncomplainingly still.

"There, that's it. Do you feel as if they could open now?"

Xenos did not answer at first and it was a little while before Philo realized that he was frightened.

"It's really fairly dark in here, you won't see much at first, particularly against the light," he said, trying to be helpful, but as scared as the man on the bed.

Xenos grimaced and slowly opened the still red eyelids part way to reveal swimming, bloodshot eyes. It seemed to hurt, because he caught his breath deep in his throat.

"Do you want to wipe them yourself?" Philo put a wet cloth into Xenos's hands. When he had finished the man turned his head so that he was looking straight at the boy. There was a moment of silence and then he said, with a voice that was part a laugh and part something else, "What made me think you had dark hair?"

"I'm brownish. Nicanor is much darker, but you haven't met him yet. Conan's fair."

Xenos raised himself on his elbow and looked around. "I thought this room was bigger. It's hard to judge noises when you can't see as well. Tell me about this house and your father."

He shut his sore eyes for most of the time that he was listening, just opening them from time to time as if to reassure himself that the lids still worked. Before Philo had quite finished Lucia came in with soup and bread.

She took one look and said, “Philo! What have you been doing?”

“Only what I asked him to. Look!” Xenos opened his eyes and smiled.

It was such a transformation that Lucia nearly dropped the bowl; beneath the scabs and the discoloured skin Xenos clearly had a handsome and sensitive face.

“The Gods be praised, and you can really see? There’s no damage?”

“I don’t know, things are still smudgy, but I can see you and the boy and the light of day outside.”

“Then you must be ready for supper,” she said, practically, seeing the emotion very near the surface, and that Xenos was not strong enough yet to cope with it. “Philo, you can feed our guest as you aren’t doing anything else useful.”

Xenos was tired now. After they had finished he lay quietly while Philo tidied the bed, and then in the strong light that was now striking directly in through the door he raised his arms and looked at the peeling skin.

“Am I like this all over?”

Philo drew back the cover for him to see. Xenos looked at his own body dispassionately. “It looks even worse than it feels. Thank heaven no one waited to turn me over when I was baked on one side!”

Without taking much notice Philo had been aware of hoofbeats outside in the road; suddenly the racket erupted into the storeyard. He heard Esdras and then Conan calling urgently for his father. He covered Xenos quickly and ran outside and up the steps. His two brothers had just dismounted and Esdras was leading away the best mule and the donkey that Conan had taken to bring Nicanor back on. The older boy looked flustered, standing with his arm round the younger's shoulders, and on Nicanor's face was an expression that Philo had never seen before.

Apollodorus strode from the front courtyard and took in the scene at a glance.

"Nico, you haven't been hurt?"

Nicanor shook his head but did not speak. His face was frozen into a blank mask of grief, his eyes red-rimmed as if he had cried for a long time. His father led them through to the family living-room.

"Conan, what happened?" Apollodorus asked.

"As far as I can make out it was the horses. Cousin Chares's farm was still in an uproar when I got there. It seemed that a quarter-master from the new depot came out with a cavalry detail yesterday afternoon looking for remounts. You know Chares's broodstock, the mares the dealers come for from Damascus? They've all gone except for two who were out on a training run. Even the little grey half-Arab who foaled five days ago. The colt was weakly, Nico sat up with him all night but he wouldn't take anything and died this morning. Then one of Chares's men brought news that they'd found the grey in the wadi below the second bridge. She must have broken away to get back to her colt, tried to jump it and missed her footing. Both her front legs were broken but the Romans hadn't stopped long enough to climb down and kill her. Chares had to do that."

"Do you remember her first colt? We sent him to the

Jerusalem horse fair, the procurator bought him—may he kick him dead!" said Nicanor quietly, looking at the floor.

Philo watched his brother helplessly. Those horses had been the most important thing in his life. Chares would get some compensation for the loss, enormous as it was, because Rome always paid in the end, but for Nicanor there was no way that this could ever be put right. The grey and her colt were dead and nothing he could say would be any use.

Then Conan went and knelt to take hold of the hands that were clenched between his brother's knees. "Come with me, come and lie down. I do understand a bit. Not horses exactly but things that can't ever be made better. It's like I felt when lightning struck the new Apollo on the temple pediment. I'd watched him being carved for months and the sculptor could never get him quite right again." Nicanor did not answer him, but he allowed himself to be led uncomplainingly away.

"Nico looks as if one of us has died, as if he was never going to get over it," said Philo, adrift on an emotion whose depth and direction he could not understand.

"I pray the Gods you may be wrong," said his father.

IV

A CLOUD OVER THE SUN

IN SPITE OF what had happened Apollodorus and Conan still left the next morning at dawn. Their business would not wait and at least the road north was safer than the desert way. It was only two days' journey and their trading might not take long, but the house was suddenly very quiet. On the first morning Philo went to school and Nicanor stayed in his room. Xenos was drowsy, in less pain, but seeming to need to sleep for a month.

Sitting on the bench at the back of the schoolroom with flies buzzing under the high ceiling and the master droning over his scrolls, Philo found it almost impossible to concentrate on his work. Xenos had been in the house four days now and it seemed that any danger that there might be talk about him in the market-place was over; the excitement over the arrival of the Romans had seen to that. Except Timon of Gerasa, no one but the servants knew where he had come from and they would not talk outside the house; they had all been with the family too long. Philo could not get the story that Xenos had told of his capture out of his head; it was getting mixed up in his mind with the quarter-Jewish part of him that he had never understood or thought about too much. When Galilee had been captured by the Romans the year before, everyone had been shocked, but they had remembered the Jewish riots and murmured that the Romans had had no choice. But now it would all happen again, soon, when the new Emperor Vitellius gave the order. Then Jerusalem would fall—and Xenos had come from there. Suddenly danger seemed very close and Philo had the feeling of chill that comes when a cloud one has not noticed covers the sun.

He walked home alone, as he always did now. The city games were over for the year and it was too hot to exercise for the fun of it. He noticed again the scars from the fighting of three years before that familiarity had made invisible. Boards were nailed across the front of the Jewish cloth-merchant's house that had never been rebuilt, and further along a broken wall surrounded a mound of rubble that in spring was a blaze of poppies. Two families had lived there, and died when a mob burned their homes down over their heads.

When he got home Lucia was sitting sewing in the courtyard on the shady western side under the colonnade and Nicanor was with her, lying back on the old couch, staring at the damp marks on the ceiling, with his hands behind his head.

As he saw her comfortable shapelessness and the bent head with the thick coil of hair streaked iron and grey Philo felt grateful for Lucia. She was there as she always had been, when his tiny dark-eyed mother was alive, and ever since her death, partly nurse and partly housekeeper. Now when Apollodorus was away the house was completely in her hands; Uncle Menelaus who lived on the other side of the hill was supposed to make important decisions but he was getting old and had never been one to disturb his weak digestion with other people's problems.

Philo dropped his school tablets on the paving stones,

kicked off his sandals and sat down on the end of the couch.

Lucia greeted him, glanced up to give him the quick experienced look that would confirm that all was well, and then put down her needle.

"What's that frown about? You weren't beaten?"

Philo wriggled. "Would I be sitting here if I had been? No, not quite. Nicanor, are you in the mood to look at my homework?"

It was one of his brother's obliging days, it seemed. Nicanor rolled over and untied the scroll, and they sat for a while, heads close together.

Lucia watched them, still wondering what had put the frown between Philo's eyebrows. He had always been the easiest of the boys, not as clever as Conan, but liking to please people, too young to feel his mother's death as badly as his elder brothers had. She let her worn hands with the twisted knuckles rest in her lap. The pain in her joints was worse today, perhaps the autumn rains would be earlier than usual. Mainly she was remembering her dead mistress, so that her heart jumped painfully when Philo's voice broke into her thoughts.

"Father doesn't often talk about Mother now, and when he does it's never anything about her being a Jew; why, Lucia?"

"Philo, you gave me a start. What made you ask that?"

"I don't know. Something Xenos said, I suppose. I don't know very much about Jews really."

"I suppose not, it's not an easy thing to understand from the outside," said Lucia. "It's something to do with a God and something to do with being a nation, and far more than just who your parents were."

Nicanor was watching her intently; with his dark eyes and dark curly hair he was very like his mother, except that the stubborn expression was all his own.

"But Mother had a Greek father, didn't she? She came from Scythopolis, and that's one of the ten cities," he said.

"But being a Jew comes from the mother, not the father, to start with. That, and then the way you live, till you're old enough to take it on yourself. There are traditions, and rules and customs; it binds you as tight as a fly in a spider's web. Without all that you're nothing, a lost sheep, they'd call you—cut off from the house of Israel. Someone who no longer lives as a Jew is considered much worse than a Gentile born outside the law who never knew any better."

"But Mother was never a Jew like that," said Philo.

"No, only when she was very small. Did you never hear all this? Nicanor, did she not tell you herself?"

"No," said Nicanor, his eyes suddenly very dark and shuttered. "She only talked about what happened after she met Father, always Father. It was as if her life began then."

"In a way I suppose it did. Her childhood was so sad. You see, her own mother died of fever when she was very small, and everyone in the house with her except the child. That was how she came to be brought up in a Greek home, her father's brother took her; I was a young girl in his kitchen then. She was such a tiny child, and it had been such a long time since there had been a child in that house, they didn't know what to do. So they got me to look after her—I was one of six."

"Poor Mother," said Philo.

"She didn't miss what she didn't know," said Lucia, folding her sewing. "But I'm glad she never saw the riots three years ago."

There seemed nothing more to say. The old woman got up and hobbled painfully towards the kitchen, and they watched her go.

"Her legs are getting worse," said Nicanor. "If she was a horse I should know what to do, but she won't let anyone help her. I've tried."

If Nicanor could mention horses he must be feeling better; Philo felt a weight lift from his heart, as if something he had only half seen had moved further away again. He got down off the end of the couch.

"Lucia won't have time for a while, I must see if Xenos needs anything. Come and talk to him, Nicanor, you never have."

He thought his brother was going to refuse, but it seemed that he could not think of a reason, so he followed Philo across the courtyard.

Xenos was lying propped up in bed with his eyes shut, for they were still very weak, but his voice when he heard them come in was nearly normal.

"Philo? I wondered where you were today."

"This is Nicanor, you haven't seen him before; he helped carry you in."

Xenos opened his eyes fully and looked up at the boy. "Thank you. I've heard your voice, and Philo said you were the dark-haired one." He smiled the smile that transformed his disfigured face.

Philo could see that his brother had the look that always reminded him of an unbroken colt sniffing an unfamiliar hand. Nicanor glanced around him as if trying to find an excuse to escape.

"Are you thirsty? This water's warm!" He picked up the jug and went back into the courtyard.

Xenos noticed Philo's disappointment. "Don't worry, not everyone makes friends as quickly as you do!" Philo blushed. "No, you do!"

The boy changed the subject quickly. "When will your eyes be strong enough to read?" he asked.

"I don't know, soon I expect, though they get tired easily. Why?"

"It was only that you seemed the sort of person who would like to read and I wondered if it would help you not to be bored. I can tell you've done a lot of writing."

"How?" Then Xenos looked at his right hand. "Oh, I see, I've got a writing bump. You're probably right. Could you find me some tablets?"

Philo went to bring his own. When he came back Xenos had propped himself over on his left elbow and was looking thoughtfully at his own hands. "It's funny, I think I know what my writing's like but I'm not sure."

Philo smoothed out the last of a half-done exercise with the blunt end of his stylus, and spread the tablets on the edge of the mattress.

"What shall I write?" Xenos asked, looking up and smiling.

"Write me a letter, I've never had one."

"To Philokles, son of Apollodorus, greetings . . ."

It came out so easily as Philo bent over to watch. Even in wax Xenos's writing was the neatest he had ever seen, on parchment it would be better than copying standard. But half-way through Xenos put the stylus down suddenly and leaned back against the pillows with his eyes shut.

"What's the matter?" Philo asked, rescuing the tablets, which were sliding underneath him. "Do you feel faint?"

"No, not exactly," he said, not opening his eyes. "It was

just that it felt—so familiar, that I was doing what I usually did. I've written hundreds of letters. It was as if for a moment I was almost back there, back doing what I used to do, but it's gone again now."

"You write very well, much better than the letter-writer down in the market."

That made him open his eyes again. "Do you think I could get work like that here in Philadelphia, even if it wasn't much? It will be some time before my eyes are strong enough to work for long. But I've been feeling like a blind puppy; I suppose they come into the world with even less than rescued travellers. I haven't even a tunic to put on when I'm well enough to get up, or a single coin to give to a servant who is kind. It's a very naked feeling."

"But Father's got lots of old tunics, though I think he's a bit taller than you. We're glad we found you, you don't have to pay us."

"Philo, that isn't the point, don't you see? It's not that I've got to pay for things, it's just that it would be helpful to me if I could. There's not much of my life I can control at the moment."

Nicanor came back with the dripping water jug. "Lucia says she forgot the parsley and could you run down to the market and see if there's any left?" he said.

Philo sighed; it was still very hot outside. He gave Xenos his drink and when he left the room his brother came with him, as if he were frightened to be left alone with the sick man.

Apollodorus returned from the north three days later. The house was running smoothly and the burns on Xenos's body were beginning to heal; Lucia's herb lore had been successful. Nicanor was now sufficiently himself again to make rude remarks to his older brother, whose fair skin was peeling badly from the sun, but who looked suddenly older and more assured.

It was a tradition in the family that the full story of a journey was never told until after dinner, and when Lucia had cleared away the three sons gathered round their father.

"I must tell you things were not easy in Gerasa," said Apollodorus, looking at his younger children. "It was the pearls mainly; spices always sell. But pearls, there must be real money about for them. The profit was nothing like what it should have been. I'm afraid I shall have to go south again almost at once, although it's getting late in the season, and there won't be as much money to leave with Lucia as I'd hoped."

"Will Conan go with you again?" asked Philo.

"No, there's too much for him to do here. I'm leaving instructions about the disposal of the rest of the goods, it's got to be done gradually or the price will come down. I've had to borrow far more than I like from Paulinus, and Conan must keep an eye on that too."

"It's a pity we have an extra mouth to feed, if we're going to be suddenly poor," said Nicanor.

"I don't understand you."

"The sick man, Xenos. What is Conan to do with him when he's recovered if he hasn't got his memory back?"

"He was asking if he could do some copying work, he writes like a professional secretary," said Philo earnestly.

"Nicanor, when have I given any sign that Xenos is not a welcome guest in my house? It is not your business to worry about the cost of his food!"

Nicanor shrugged his shoulders, but his face stayed calm; it was Philo who blushed for him.

"I think we can leave that to him. He may well prove to have friends he can write to. But let me make this plain—Philo named him Xenos and he is a guest guided here by a God, I am certain of that. And I have too often in the desert owed my life to another man's water bottle or spare camel, or to the goodwill of the strangers one meets for one night at a camp fire, not to give all he needs to a man I judge to be brave and kind."

They talked a little longer about the route he would take and the length of the journey; then Lucia put the lamps out and the boys went to bed.

As he often did Philo talked to Nicanor, leaning against the doorpost of the room his older brothers shared.

"Why did you say that, about Xenos?" asked Philo. "It made you sound so selfish. Don't you mind about people or is it only animals?"

"Someone had to ask, I was only being practical. And we don't know who he is and what he's really done. He might be a spy or anything."

Philo did not trust himself to answer and it seemed that Nicanor understood the silence only too well, because he went on again after a while. "Besides, it is a dangerous time for Father to be away from Philadelphia. Don't you think I shall miss him too, when he's away? It hurts me as well, only I have a different way of showing it. You can hang around Xenos and have long talks with him. I can't, it wouldn't work."

"All right, don't go on. But Xenos would like to talk to you if you'd let him."

Nicanor had been washing, bent over the bowl of water. He straightened up and snorted into his towel as he dried himself, then he said very quietly. "But his face! I don't know how you can bear to touch him! The Romans did that to him, and he bore it all, and he doesn't complain. I know he's brave, but when I see him I feel sick. Didn't you understand?"

V

THE FIFTY-FOURTH DAY

XENOS CAME very slowly across the courtyard leaning on Conan's arm, a thin young man in a long tunic with his face still scarred and discoloured from his burns, though his hair and beard were now neatly trimmed. His wounds were nearly healed but his body still seemed drained of strength and he could only walk with difficulty because his left leg was swollen. Behind his back Lucia had often pursed her lips and wondered if her first fears were right and he would never recover fully. She was especially afraid that the dreams that came at night, to wake him lost in a wild darkness of pain and terror, might never leave him.

Philo noticed from the dark shadows under Xenos's eyes that he had still not fully recovered from the most recent of those nights.

"Come and sit here." He arranged the cushions on the couch. "I can't do my homework."

Xenos eased himself down and lay back with his eyes shut. "I'll answer any questions I can but don't ask me to read anything. I've worked for too long on the copy of the Satires of Horace for the archon and my eyes feel as if they're burnt out for good."

"You know you oughtn't to do so much. Honestly, Xenos, anyone would think you were saving up to buy your freedom!"

Conan raised his eyebrows at his brother and pulled a face, and no one said anything for a while. Then Philo, in a small voice said, "I'm sorry, that was silly. I suppose in a way you are."

"Yes, I thought you might see that for yourself," said Xenos, who did not seem annoyed. "Of course I don't need the money at the moment, but who knows what I shall need, when . . . the great when, if it comes."

"Money for a journey?" asked Conan.

"Probably just that. One of the few things I'm sure about is that I don't come from Philadelphia, or someone would have claimed me by now. I may remember duties that are long overdue and need to make a rapid journey."

"If the roads are safe."

"Yes, always supposing that, and that I'm well enough. Now, what about this homework. Latin or Greek?"

Latin was a skill which had to be mastered for business, not conversation or pleasure, but Xenos had discovered that he spoke it as easily as the boys did their native Greek, and Philo was exceptionally quick with languages anyway. When the immediate problem had been solved Xenos opened his eyes and caught Philo looking at him.

"What is it? Is there something else?"

"It's something rather peculiar. I've been wondering for a long time if I should tell you, if it would help or upset you."

"If it's important, and you seem to think it is, perhaps we should find out."

Philo had started now and could not back out, so he began in a rush. "From the beginning we've found out things about you that you didn't know yourself. There's something else you haven't been able to see. Do you remember about your back?"

"What about it?"

"Only that once, some time ago, you've had a very bad flogging."

"Long ago?"

"Yes, I don't know, perhaps five years. The scars are quite white and starting to fade. But it must have been a proper flogging, they're very level and there are a lot of them."

"Worse than anything you've had, and not done by a bad-tempered schoolmaster! I see."

Xenos shut his eyes again and leaned his head back. Philo thought he was quite calm until he noticed that his fingers had clenched round the end of the couch.

"You remember the time you told us what happened that night on the pass to Macherus? You said then—something strange, that I've wondered about—about the pain, that it was as if it had all happened before and could happen again. Like a dream that keeps coming back."

"Did I say that? I can't remember anything about telling you what happened. It was early on, wasn't it?"

He sat up painfully and bent forward so that his face was hidden, his hand picking at the fringe of a cushion. "My family, whatever family I had, they're so much a blank that I think I can never have had one. Perhaps I was a slave, perhaps I still am, an escaped slave."

"No, you don't talk like one. They all sound different, even the clever ones," said Conan.

"Thank you, but then why was I beaten?" He wriggled his shoulder-blades as if trying to remember the forgotten scars. "I was clearly not a citizen or I wouldn't have been. It's almost more of a puzzle than it was before. I think there must have been friends, even if there was no family, and work, and some reason for me to be in Galilee or Judaea.

But in the centre of it all there is still the great emptiness that has been there from the first moment when I woke in the dark and felt your hands and heard your voices. 'What do I believe, what have I lived by all my life, what sort of man am I?' It's more important than the name of my best friend or the crime for which I was punished."

He turned back to them suddenly. "My friend!" His face seemed to light up and then the animation sank again like the flare when a wick has failed to light. "Something, someone almost came then." He raised a hand and let it fall. "Conan, will you help me? It's not as warm as I'd thought."

They walked slowly back across the courtyard and disappeared through the door.

"Philo," said Conan when he came back, "you took a chance."

"It's his back, he had a right to know. I thought it might help."

"Perhaps it has, even if it doesn't show yet. He'll go back and think and think now, and it may be like a stiff key, you try it several ways before it opens the lock."

"Floodgate, more likely. I was suddenly afraid it would all come out and we wouldn't know what to do," said Philo.

"If only Father was here. How long has he been gone? Fifty-three days, isn't it? It could be another twenty before he gets back and so much could have happened by then. And the rains will have made the roads bad."

Alone in his room Xenos, the stranger even to himself, lay on his back with his hands behind his head. The stiff leg still throbbed and there was a place across his stomach where the thin scar skin kept cracking and the raw places itched. Otherwise he was not at the moment so much uncomfortable as tired, with the weariness and weakness that never seemed to leave him. He was glad the boy had told him, although he knew that now there would be more hours during the long nights when the absence of memory would plague him, and he would wake from a nightmare not knowing if it was true or if Philo's words had fed it into his mind.

He sat up and undid the shoulder-clasps of his borrowed tunic so that it slid down. No, there was no way he could see his back, but now he knew that they were there he could feel the low ridges across his shoulders. He eased himself back on to the bed, instinctively turning on to his stomach which he had not done for a long time, with his face in the pillow. And his eyes were wet, not because he had strained them with work but because he knew how it had felt when he had lain like this before, and there was a voice and a joy mixed with the pain he had been feeling that did not make any sense to him now. But the voice was the clearest thing about it, young yet full of authority, a voice that was very important to him saying, 'I wouldn't have told you now if I'd thought it would upset you. I only wanted to give you something good to think about before you slept.' So there had been a friend, he had guessed truly, and perhaps sleep would give him back fully to the unfurnished loneliness of his mind.

The next day was a holiday. There was a cold wind from the north that sent white clouds scudding across a sky of a far paler blue than had hung above the city all summer; it was a day for walking rather than sitting in the courtyard. Philo was glad enough when Lucia found him an errand down to the market. Conan had already gone out early to meet his friend Jason, and Nicanor was with his cousin Chares on his farm to the north of the city. He had not spoken of the dead mare for some time, but Philo knew she was not forgotten. Nicanor was recovered enough to go back to working with those animals that were left, but no one could tell what the shock had really meant to him. He had not talked about it, and it was as if he had pushed the very memory of it down deep into his mind.

Lucia did not trust the kitchen-girl with any except the simplest errands, and with Conan too important now and Nicanor away she had a habit of keeping Philo busy. It was coloured thread she needed this time. He had a hank to match, so it was not difficult, and he quickly found what he wanted at one of the little shops in the arches at the back of the arcade that edged the market-place. He stowed it away in his wallet and walked over to the fountain in the middle to see if he could find any of his friends.

"Were you looking for your brother?" asked a young man who was a former school friend of Conan's.

"No, not really."

"I saw him just now with the son of Eupolemus."

"He's old enough to choose his own friends," said Philo uncomfortably, trying to edge away. This had been going on for more than a month, ever since, partly occupied with his father's business, Conan had given up his studies and had more time on his hands. But this friendship with Jason the son of Eupolemus had been bad news to the family. Although the young man was handsome and amusing he was no friend for anyone who needed to watch what money he spent and yet loved fine things as Conan had always done. Suddenly, even more than usual, Philo wished that his father was home again.

He turned back towards the steep road that led round the eastern slope of the citadel towards home, but before he had left the market-place he heard his own name called twice in a voice that he knew, loud enough to cut through the market racket and yet in some way unfamiliar.

He turned and saw Conan there, in the centre of a small group of men, a cluster clearly marked out from the indolence of the stall-holders and loungers by their grave faces and the way that they surrounded his brother as if he was something fragile and about to break. Philo ran back down the slope towards him, thinking he must be suddenly ill, or that Nicanor had had an accident. People stopped what they were doing to turn and watch him, so that when he reached the group at the edge of the square they were the centre of a large and inquisitive crowd.

Conan's face was an odd colour, pasty beneath the normal tan. The hands he was trying to keep at his sides were shaking, he looked round despairingly at the ring of faces.

"Philo, come home with me now. Not here, but I must tell you . . ."

But a voice behind his shoulder, that sounded like Paulinus at his most unctuous, said, "Look at the poor child, only fourteen, what an age to become an orphan!"

The word did not mean anything. From the first moment that he had seen Conan's face Philo had known that something had gone, one of those things had happened which change the future and set it off in a different direction. But he was still thinking of Nicanor and some stupid or painful accident that would be difficult to cope with while his father was away. Then—it seemed a long while after—in the time it took to cover the last five paces, his mind pulled him up short with the lurch that comes when one has slept for just a moment. Father! That was what orphan meant, a child without a father!

Conan swung round angrily, but it was too late, the word had been spoken and Philo caught at his arm stammering, his face dissolving as a smacked child's does, suddenly crimson, the tears spurting from his eyes. Conan did the only thing he could to hide what he saw in that face and what the crowd could see; he pulled his young brother close to him, wrapped a fold of his cloak round him and began to lead him up the hill towards home.

The crowd fell back, and only the men who had known Apollodorus well were there by the time they had turned the last corner. Philo was quieter now, so Conan stopped and held him further away, speaking as gently as he could.

"Paulinus told me too, he had it from a caravan leader just up from the south. It was in the last mountains before the sea at Eilat. Robbers he said, and Father died fighting. It must have been ten days ago, he thinks Esdras was killed as well. It was at night."

Philo wiped his face on his brother's cloak and drew a deep hiccupping breath. He would not give the watching men the satisfaction of seeing any more of his grief. The numbness of a severe wound was already coming over him. This he could not accept now; he had been told it, slowly he would understand, but meanwhile he must think, not feel. There was the household to think about, and Nicanor, more than Conan could possibly cope with alone.

At the door of the house Conan suddenly turned on the men who were still with them, thanked them for their concern, hoped to see them later and then got himself and his brother inside the house alone with the gate shut behind them.

Xenos was working in his room and Lucia was standing in the doorway talking to him. She had turned, hearing the voices outside the gate, and something in the sound of them to make her feel uneasy. At the sight of Conan's face her hands went to her mouth.

Conan, looking suddenly very like his father, was gentle with her; he put an arm round her shoulders and pushed her through the doorway of Xenos's room and sat her down on the bed. The man looked up from the table at which he had been writing and put his pen down very deliberately and slowly.

"Conan, what's happened?"

Conan sat down on the bed beside Lucia and took her twisted hands in his. "It's Father. Paulinus heard."

"The master's been hurt?" From her eyes Lucia already understood, but she said it all the same.

Conan shook his head. "It was in the mountains near Eilat ten days ago; robbers, we don't know any more." Then it was he who put his head on her shoulder and her arms came around him, while she patted and clucked as she had when he was a little boy with a grazed knee.

Philo was standing in the doorway. Everything seemed far away, as if there were a barrier between him and the other people in the room. Conan's sobbing was a very long way off and within himself was the beginning of a pain so deep that he struggled to keep it back, terrified of losing himself under the weight of it. He started to shiver.

Xenos had been sitting with his head bowed. He got up carefully and looked at the boy. "This is certain?"

"Conan says so."

Xenos stood close to him but did not touch him. Philo wiped a hand across his face and said, "Nico! I shall have to go."

Xenos opened his mouth to protest and then shut it

again. It was too much to ask of Philo, but who else was there to send? Conan could not go yet, and anyway as the eldest he should stay in the house. The business of death did not allow much time for grieving.

Conan shook himself and sat up. "Take the mule and try to bring him back; we should be together."

Philo turned and went out without a word. Looking after him Xenos remembered Apollodorus, for the man he had been, not only as the father of his children. And this good man, now dead, had saved his life at some risk to his own and brought him into his home. Apollodorus himself had said that a God must have moved him to it; could it be that the purpose behind that action was now plain? Xenos felt weariness that was not only in his body, and yet at the same time something that was not yet quite hope, but more a relief that the future was not quite so shapeless as he had imagined.

VI

THE RECKONING

PHILO BROUGHT Nicanor back at the hour when the last colour had left the sky, and Cousin Chares came with them. They found Conan already sitting in the dining-room with Uncle Menelaus, Paulinus and two other merchants. Xenos was in the corner of the room with his head bent. In the pauses in the conversation they could hear the sobbing of the kitchen-girl in the far courtyard.

Conan was composed now, feeling unreal, as if he was acting a part; he had heard himself greet Paulinus and the others and discuss what rites it would be possible to carry out for his father, as there was no chance of the body being found. Then there was a pause. Philo seemed completely exhausted, as well he might be, and Nicanor had hardly spoken. Already weary himself, Conan had no idea how he was going to cope with his brother after the men had gone, for he could sense that of all the difficulties that faced the family this would be the worst. Their father's death was one fact that even Nicanor could not make go away by ignoring it.

But the men showed no signs of going either and Paulinus was even trying to talk business.

"You know that your father borrowed considerable sums of money from me before he left? It is too soon to be sure, of course, but it would seem that what he took with him must be counted as utterly lost. This will put us all in an awkward position."

Philo, watching his brother's strained face, wondered if Paulinus wanted his money that very evening. It all began to feel even more dreamlike. Conan twitched as if he had been almost asleep, and drew himself upright.

"Gentlemen, in the morning we must make the offerings for my father. After that, noble Paulinus, it would be a kindness if you could collect together an account of all that my father owed, and when we have the amount before us we can arrange for its payment."

"But my boy . . ." twittered the old uncle.

Conan silenced him and surprised the others by standing up. Reluctantly Paulinus and the merchants rose with him, and then found themselves being ushered out to the gate.

Conan walked back slowly to the dining-room. Cousin Chares was still sitting miserably next to old Menelaus; he was a big man with a face the colour of Roman brick.

"Conan, what will you do?" he asked. "You know how I'm placed; since I lost the mares I haven't two coins to rub together. I can't sell the farm. As for Nicanor, there's always work for him since my own boy died. But more than that, three of you . . . do you know what the debt will be?" His hands were rubbing together helplessly.

Conan caught his younger brother's eye and Nicanor jerked himself up from a pit of silence. "We all know you'll do what you can, don't worry, cousin. Now, can you get back to the farm tonight, it's very late?"

The big man got up awkwardly and looked around him at the shabby, comfortable room. "Perhaps I should stay with you."

"Cousin, it's the fifty-fourth night since our father left us, we're used to being alone," said Conan quietly.

It was arranged that Chares should spend the night with the old uncle. While Nicanor was seeing them out Philo said, "But you know, the house does feel more empty. We always knew before, or we hoped . . ." He could not finish, but Xenos understood.

He got up slowly and went out into the dark courtyard. Conan and Nicanor were standing by the gate and Lucia came through from the kitchen, shielding the tiny lamp in her hands from the chilly night wind.

"I've just got that silly girl quiet, I think; now, my poor boys, you must rest yourselves. Come on now, Philo, you're dropping on your feet, go to bed."

"But, Xenos, what are we going to do? Shouldn't we try to make a plan?"

"Do what Lucia says," he said gently. "What can you decide tonight? You must rest even if you can't sleep. I've been watching and thinking; tomorrow this first day at least will be behind you." He turned into his own doorway.

Conan saw Philo standing, drooping and uncertain; he put an arm round his shoulders. "Come on then, we don't any of us want to be alone. You can come in with me as long as you don't kick."

Xenos, lying fully dressed on his bed, heard their voices for a little longer and then the house was quiet. He knew that it would be a long time before he slept himself; he tried to calculate in his mind what the contents of the house were worth, the beasts, the last of the stock from Apollodorus's journey. There was probably some of his wife's jewellery too, waiting to be given as a gift to Conan's bride. Xenos noticed that he still seemed to know what things were worth. Everything would depend on the important figure that Paulinus would bring the next day.

But even after the debts were met what would the boys live on? Chares had been right to see the difficulty there. Nicanor seemed for once to be luckiest of the three; school would have to stop for Philo, and how would Conan occupy himself, in so small a city where he had always till now had money and position as well as his good looks? They must, if it was at all possible, keep the house, but could they afford to live there? He dozed and woke and dozed again, and then as the first cocks of Philadelphia crying into the still black sky broke again into his shallow sleep the stirrings of an idea came to him.

Philo woke first in the room where the boys were sleeping together. Only a wan greyness showed in the sky and the cover had slipped further than he could reach. Conan lay half across him, still asleep; they had crowded two in a bed as they had when he was very small and afraid of the dark, seeking what comfort there was in physical nearness. But it had been Nicanor who had cried himself to sleep, under the covers, hoping that the others could not hear. Philo felt his own head ache now with unshed tears.

He managed to ease himself from under Conan's spread arm; it sounded as if someone was stirring. As he went out into the strange grey light Xenos was standing in his doorway.

"Is Conan awake?" he asked quietly.

"He wasn't just now." Philo turned back into the room and saw that Conan's eyes were open. He beckoned to him, glancing across at the sleeping hump of Nicanor.

The light was strong enough now for them to see each

other's faces as they huddled side by side on Xenos's bed. "Conan, I think you may have to think quickly and see clearly, or you will find yourselves forced into accepting help you don't want. Do you understand that?"

"I know I'd rather be miserable doing something I've chosen, than sit meekly in Paulinus's warehouse and be grateful for every meal I ate," said Conan.

"I thought you might feel like that. Now, do you know what the most valuable possession you have is?" Then Xenos's heart ached, because Conan had looked at once at his younger brother. No, he thought, after your family. Aloud he said, "This house. It's well situated, better than many in the city, the stables are good. If you let it you would have enough to live on, enough for you three."

"And Lucia," said Philo.

"Yes, and Lucia. Old Atius and the two girls are slaves, you'll have to sell them."

"And there must be room for you." From Philo Xenos would have expected it, but not from Conan and he was so moved that for the moment he was speechless.

"You can't leave us now, not yet, even if your memory comes back today and your strength with it," said Conan urgently. "You wouldn't, would you? You're right about the house, I suppose it is one way out, but where would we live ourselves?"

"There are the storerooms off the yard. We wouldn't need much space, if only we didn't have to go altogether. I don't think I could bear to go on living in Philadelphia and pass the door of this house and know there were only strangers here," said Philo.

"But who would they be? Who in Philadelphia could afford to live here?" asked Conan.

"I don't know, we mustn't try to go too fast. By tonight we shall be seeing things more clearly," said Xenos.

Philo went back into his room next door and dressed slowly. He remembered the rites for his father and put on his best tunic and then had to hunt for his newest sandals. He had hardly worn them but they were already almost too small. He sat down on the bed that had not been slept in and looked around the room almost as if when he left it that morning he would not be coming back. It would be easier if it could be like that, and not drawn out as he knew it must be. He felt heavy and cold and already tired, with an ache in his heart that went on and on dully like toothache. He was still trying to make himself think of what lay ahead as just something unpleasant that had to be gone through, like having the aching tooth pulled, not anything to do with a father whom he had loved and who would now never stride through the gate again.

That second day was the worst, with the funeral offerings and the procession of callers, and then Paulinus with his tablets and his good advice. When he had gone and the figure was known Conan and Xenos went round the house checking and making lists. The day after that, like a gift from the gods Timon of Gerasa arrived, their father's friend, and it was he who saw to the selling of the slaves for them, and who himself, in memory of Apollodorus, bought what they could not easily get rid of in Philadelphia. More could not be expected of him.

When there was something practical to do Nicanor was helpful enough, but he made no suggestions and seemed not quite to understand where all Conan's plans were leading. It was on the seventh day, when Timon had ridden north again, that the final decision could be delayed no longer. The dining-room furniture had gone and so they sat on the beds in the boys' room, with Lucia in the chair Conan had kept because it was easy for her stiff knees, waiting for Conan who had been out on important business.

When his brother came in Philo noticed that for the first time since their father's death there was a little colour in his face. He had been hurrying and that could only mean he had been successful. It was difficult to know whether to be glad or not.

"Xenos, you were right, they're coming to look anyway," Conan said, throwing himself down on the bed.

"Who's coming?" asked Nicanor, suddenly suspicious, and raising himself from his lethargy.

"Nico, I didn't tell you before because I knew it would upset you and there was no point if it wasn't going to happen. You know—we've discussed it—that we have to let the house. It's all right for you, you can go back to the farm, but we, the rest of us, have got to have somewhere to live."

"I know you have, I'm not stupid."

"But do you know how difficult it is to find someone to take the house, with the war on and things so difficult? Though I suppose it's only because of the war that Xenos, we that is, had the idea."

"What idea?" Nicanor looked suspiciously across at Xenos. As the days had passed his awkwardness with the man had grown less, but he still kept away from him as much as possible, even though the burns were fading.

"I've just been down to the Roman camp. No, let me finish. We thought there was a strong chance they might soon need somewhere more comfortable to use as an officers' mess, when they had visitors, something like that. There are often high-ranking officers passing through. There's a tribune in charge, left behind because he's recovering from a leg wound. I was taken to him. He liked the sound of the house, and they're coming tomorrow to look."

Nicanor stood up slowly, "You mean Romans, here, in these rooms, while you sleep in a store-shed?"

Suddenly furious, Philo shouted, "Where are we to sleep, then? In a stable with you? Even Lucia? What did you think was going to happen? Have you got a better idea—we haven't had any suggestions from you so far. All the time when Conan and Xenos have been working so hard!"

"Xenos! Why pretend it's Conan's idea? Very well, I understand now. I won't live under the same roof with a Roman, you never thought I would, did you? If this is your way of trying to get rid of me, it's worked. I don't expect you'll need to know where to find me, but you do—to start with anyway."

He was already on his feet. Now he turned and pulled down his cloak from the wall and began to pile tunics and old sandals on to it. Lucia got up and went to him.

"Nicanor, please don't, let me do that. Don't go off like this. Think what your father would have wanted!"

At that Nicanor started crying, but he would not stop what he was doing. Philo watched him, frozen with shock and distress, while he fastened his bundle and ran out into the courtyard without saying good-bye. The front gate slammed shut and then the house was very quiet.

Lucia, whom none of them could ever remember having seen cry, sat down heavily with the tears running down her face. "Let me go away, Conan. I've got friends in the city, one of them would take me. You're only doing this for me. Don't let him go like that."

Conan went to her and took her hands. "Dear Lucia, no. You are part of our family and while one of us is left in Philadelphia you live with us. Let's hear no more of that. It isn't why Nicanor ran away—because that is what he's doing. I don't like Romans either, but what does he want me to do—hire myself out as a donkey-boy? Xenos said the first night that we had to see things clearly; the difference is that Philo and I want to and Nicanor won't even try."

The words had been said and they were true, but that did not make the pain any easier. Philo went quietly away and began to move the first of his things through into the storeyard, Lucia and Xenos followed him, and Conan was left alone to look at his brother's deserted bed.

Next morning the Romans came. Philo reported to Lucia, who was keeping out of sight in the kitchen. "They're on the far side looking at the stables now."

Lucia looked up from the onions she was peeling. "Do they look pleased?"

"I think so. The tribune's there, he has black hair and I think he's the one Conan saw with Father on the first day when the legate came. And there's a centurion who looks fat and bad-tempered and a clerk who's writing down everything Conan says."

"I thought your uncle was supposed to be showing them round?"

"Yes, he's there, but I don't think he was doing it very well, so Conan took over. It was partly his idea."

The sound of voices outside moved back into the main courtyard and Philo went back towards the steps. Although it was still morning the house had an afternoon hush about it. The bareness and tidiness already belonged to somewhere that was not being lived in; there was a pile of bundles already carried through and waiting to be arranged, but the stables opposite were empty and there was no bustle from the servants, or distant humming as the kitchen-girl washed the flagstones in the dining-room. Suddenly he was afraid to go down to the empty rooms where he had lived all his life.

Conan came up through the archway, carrying a cage with Lucia's singing-bird.

"We forgot him, he was hanging in the colonnade and the tribune noticed! Yes, they're coming. We're going to keep this side of the yard and have a fence put up so we won't be stared at. Come and help me move the beds."

By evening it was all done. There were two rooms, a small one for Lucia with a lean-to outside where she would cook, and a larger one with two beds, one for Conan and Philo and the other for Xenos. They were crowded with bundles, the walls were only roughly plastered and there was hardly room for Xenos to set up his copying table, but they were still home and with winter upon them at least they could keep each other warm. As Philo carried the last basket through from the courtyard he heard the sound of people passing outside in the road and the shrilling of flutes. It was possibly a wedding, but echoing in the empty courtyard the music was thin and eerie, more like a funeral, the funeral they had not been able to give his father. And with that sound it seemed that the end came to the childhood he had spent in the house.

Next morning Conan hired two men to put up the fence in the storeyard. The ground was iron hard and by the time they had dug the post-holes the little rooms were gritty with dust and the Romans had arrived—loud voices from the front of the house and strange horses being led through the back gate into the stables. Xenos kept out of the way, although he knew that there was no chance that with his scarred face he would be recognized by anyone who had seen him in the desert. After he had welcomed the tribune Conan went out, certain that he had done what was best for the family and yet hating to see and hear it happen. When he came back late in the afternoon Philo was on his hands and knees trying to get the fire to go; he sat back on his heels, with a smudge of dirt across his cheek and grinned.

"I've got a job!"

"You've what?" Conan noticed that it was the first time since the fifty-fourth day that he had seen his younger brother smile.

"I'm going to work for the tribune, Marius Gallienus, for the Romans. I went and asked, and he looked me up and down and said they needed a boy to run errands who knew the city, and to wait at table. At least I shall get my meals."

Xenos, hearing what was going on and coming to the doorway, saw Conan go red with anger. "Steady," he said. "If things had worked out badly and there hadn't been enough money even if you'd sold the house, you might have been slaves by now, both of you, and doing worse things than serving at table."

It was true and that truth was so appalling that Conan felt himself go cold and his anger drain away.

"Sorry," he said. "That was clever of you, Philo, and good luck to you. I suppose I'm jealous, at least you'll have something to do."

He went through into their room and began to stack his belongings more tidily. Xenos, looking after him, gave him a little while on his own. It had been so quick; only that summer the boy had been a law student, now he was envying his brother a servant's job. Yet thank the Gods for Philo; he had loved his father deeply and this loss could have crushed him utterly, and yet now he was blowing up the fire again and making jokes with Lucia. He was the youngest, and young trees bend more easily to the wind, but it was something more than that. It was too early yet to see clearly what this upturning of their lives would do to each of the sons of Apollodorus, but the beginning at least was plain.

VII

DECIMUS

IT WAS A fine night late in the winter, almost moonless, but with enough light from the cold stars to show the roofs of the houses and above them the higher walls of the citadel. Lucia was sitting with Xenos and Conan in their room, huddled round a small charcoal brazier. The tiny lamp did not give enough light for her to sew, so for once her stiff hands were quiet. It was a night like so many during the last two months when the Romans had been in the house; their cook was singing next door in the kitchen, and from the noise it sounded as if the tribune was out and the centurion Decimus was getting drunk again. There was no point in even trying to sleep yet.

"I think he's worse tonight," said Conan.

"Then it won't be long. He'll go to sleep suddenly as usual and then it will be quiet again."

Although the tribune Gallienus was in command, at first the wound that had kept him behind in Philadelphia had caused him too much pain to let him undertake the day-to-day running of the depot. The family had seen far more of Decimus, and his moods had come to have the same effect as the weather on their lives—they could not be controlled but they affected the ease or difficulty with which things could be done. Decimus did not like Philadelphia, he had been losing steadily at dice for days, and there was not enough work for his men. It had been a cold and wet winter. Most of the troops left in the city had been sick or wounded, only fit for light duties, so the centurion could not even give himself the satisfaction of the merciless drilling that would have put an edge on his command sufficient to make the legate's eye gleam if he came back this way.

Lucia cocked an ear at the noise from the other courtyard. "That was loud. Poor Philo, I hope Decimus isn't sick again."

A voice called for the centurion's batman.

"That's it," said Conan. "Bedtime all round!"

Philo, standing beside a smoking table-lamp in which a fly had just drowned, was thinking the same thing. The dining-room seemed murky, the air almost too thick to breathe, heavy with smells of meat fat, sweat and wine. A Roman dinner was so different from the dignified way his father had entertained that it was impossible to believe that it had been in the same room where he waited now as a servant.

Then Decimus's head went down among the nut-shells and grape-skins, and an almost audible sigh came from the other servants.

"Here we go again!" Two of the junior officers present hoisted the big man up and frog-marched him out into the cooler air outside.

"Right!" said Fulvius, the mess steward. "Now don't break those cups in the rush, they're genuine Corinthian and the tribune's fond of them."

But even as Philo began to load his tray there was the always ominous sound of quick hoofbeats outside in the road, and a shout at the gate. Philo put down the cup he was holding and ran out into the courtyard. No, of course that was silly, this was no homecoming, nothing that could mean anything good or bad for him. But he stayed all the same while the guard called for the officer on duty.

He came, somewhat untidy, from Decimus's quarter. A dispatch rider had ridden into the yard. "Urgent message for the tribune," he said, not dismounting.

"He's not here, he's gone out to dinner. Do we know where?" He looked around for Fulvius.

"With Eupolemus the councillor, sir," said the guard. "But I'm not sure where his house is."

Philo was tired, there was still work to do, but this might get him out of some of it. He stepped forward into the lamplight. "I know, sir."

"Thank goodness for that. If the dispatch really won't wait."

Philo went forward to take the rider's stirrup. It was a right turn out of the gateway and hard to see where to put one's feet in the dark streets. He had not often been out so late, but in this company it was safe enough, and the city was very quiet. The horse's hooves slipped on the cobbles of the steep streets in the upper part of the citadel. On the brow of the hill was a small paved square with the portico of the temple of Zeus on one side and the council chamber on the other. In the faint light the pillars of the temple were bone-white, and in the corner of the steps was a dark hump that must be the beggar who always sat there. Two stray dogs barked at their heels, and a drunken man backed against a wall; then they were going down the other side, and lights shone through the gateway of the house of Eupolemus.

There were voices just inside; the tribune and the other

guests were about to leave. The messenger swung down from his horse and threw the reins to Philo.

Marius Gallienus, swarthy, tall and only just beginning to lose his good looks, caught the flash of his helmet. "Over here, trooper."

The man saluted and handed over the scroll. "Urgent, is it?" asked the tribune, raising an eyebrow. He limped back into the light as he unrolled it. Philo looked at the messenger and realized that he had the look of gloomy satisfaction that comes with the handing on of certain sorts of bad news.

Then Gallienus made a sound, not much more than a drawing-in of the breath, and put the scroll carefully away in the breast of his dress tunic. Slowly he turned back towards his host and the other guests, still waiting uncertainly in the lighted gateway. His face showed nothing, but there was something suddenly formal about the way he held himself.

"This news has travelled fast! Gentlemen, I have to tell you that the Emperor Vitellius is with the Gods."

It was only when Philo saw the shocked faces of the men in the lamp-light that he understood that that meant "dead." But what came now? Vitellius had been the third Emperor since Nero had died the year before, names only who had come and gone so quickly that here beyond the edge of the Empire they had meant nothing. Nero had been there ever since the year Philo was born, his face was on the coins and the statues, but Galba, Otho, Vitellius—now the same wind had blown them all away and the armies would already be marching again far away in Italy. And who wore the purple now? Eupolemus was asking the tribune that.

Gallienus had a strange look on his face, as if the gravity due to the moment was losing a battle with excitement and anticipation.

"Councillor, I know no more than you. But there may be more news soon, and it could be of particular interest to us here."

Then he was in a hurry to be away, the messenger was dismissed to barracks and Philo had to run to keep up behind Gallienus and his escort, not to be left alone in the streets at night. As they neared the house he slipped off up the higher turning that led to the back wall, climbed it by a familiar ladder of rough stones and hand-holds and dropped down into the storeyard. It should certainly be possible to escape further duties that night.

The family rooms were quite quiet, and gentle snoring through the open door told him that Lucia was asleep. In the other room Xenos sat up when he came in.

"Philo? What was all that noise about? Not trouble?"

"I don't know. Is it trouble when an Emperor dies? We should be used to it by now!" He understood now how the messenger had felt.

That seemed to wake Conan too. "Vitellius?"

"Well, there's only one Emperor at the moment, isn't there?" said Philo wearily, prodding him to move over as he slid out of his tunic and sandals.

"Probably not by now," said Xenos, thoughtfully. "And this news is more than a month old. I wonder which general was nearest Rome when it happened!"

Philo asked, "Why should it make any difference to us here, to our war? They won't all suddenly leave, will they?"

"We'll know more in the morning," said Conan. Then after a silence, "Titus, the legate Vespasian's son, left for

Rome last month, I wonder if he was sniffing out how the land lay."

It was quiet in the room and Philo was almost asleep when Xenos said very softly, "I remember when Nero died, I know I was shaken by it; it's as if I knew what his voice had been like. I wonder how." It was some time now since he had said anything like that.

By an hour after dawn the next day the news was all over the city. The councillors, anxious to do the right thing, met in urgent session, ordered official mourning and had funeral wreaths put on all the statues of the Gods. The citizens enjoyed the excitement and the Romans looked solemn. Philo's fellow-servants spent most of the day discussing the donative that the new Emperor, whoever he was, would make by custom to all serving troops when he assumed the purple. Like Xenos they began to wonder which general had been nearest Rome and if he was rich.

Xenos woke in a strange mood. Usually as soon as there was room to move he set up his folding table and began the copying work that was now bringing him a small but steady income as his eyes grew stronger. Today he knew that he could not settle to any work that would be worth paying for, and Conan understood that he wanted to be on his own and went out earlier than usual.

The first month after the Romans came had been worst for Conan; Philo was busy, Xenos had his copying, but what was he to do? How could he stand about in the market-place talking to his friends, with their plans for work and study, when he had no money in his pocket and nothing to look forward to? Now he was the one who had to run Lucia's errands, and after Jason had caught him once hurrying up to the back of the house carrying two squawking hens, he had tried to keep away from the laughter and the pitying glances. He had spent some time up on the citadel hill watching the building of the new temple. That was something that had always fascinated him; he loved beautiful things, clean lines, the look of a new statue, and the stone masons had got to know him. In the yard where the capitals for the columns and the figures for the pediment were being carved he was safe from mocking eyes. For the last month he had been helping the sculptor who was making a statue of the Emperor which would stand in the square outside. So far he was not being paid, but he was coming home tired with his hair full of marble dust and sleeping better, and Lucia and Xenos had exchanged relieved glances.

"Wait a minute, don't take your cloak off," said Kleas the sculptor as Conan came into the yard. He was not a Greek, but a Syrian from Antioch with no great opinion of himself as an artist. He could produce a standard statue of a God or an Emperor and if it was not a very good likeness most people knew no better anyway.

"What do you want?" Conan asked.

"It's the drapery over the left arm. There was a fault in the stone and the edge had split off; I shall have to change it. No, stand still while I see how your cloak hangs."

It was cold standing and Conan looked longingly across at the column base he was being allowed to work on with Kleas's chisel.

"What about the news then?" asked Kleas, whistling through his teeth.

"What news? Oh, the Emperor, you mean. I suppose that's why you left the head till last. Now who will you have to put on it?"

"Ah, that's the question. And of course I left the head on purpose, I wasn't born yesterday. Got caught that way in Caesarea once. I expect the council will be along pretty quick with further orders, once they know."

He stood back and looked at the figure. "I knew a God guided me not to make him too tall, not that they notice, patrons. Make the figure tall and it shows respect. But Vespasian's only a little man and he's stocky. I'm going to have my work cut out."

"Vespasian?"

"That's what they're saying in the market, hadn't you heard? Then Titus his son'll be back here to Judaea as soon as it's safe to sail, and I wouldn't be a Jew in Jerusalem by midsummer for all the corn in Egypt. All right, I've got it now, you can get on with your work."

Conan had only been working long enough to warm himself up when there was the sound of voices in the gateway to the yard. Even with his back turned he recognized Eupolemus the councillor. The regular chinking of hammers from the other masons stopped, but Conan kept his head down, crouching over his work. He had heard Jason's laugh.

It was as Kleas had expected, tactful orders to carry on with the other work till the city was sure. Then a shadow fell across the dusty stone-chipped ground where Conan was kneeling.

"It can't be! Why, Conan, is this where you're hiding?" Jason, tall and beautifully dressed, was at his most charming, but already the story as it would be told in the scent shop in the market later that morning was being embroidered in his mind.

Conan stood up and dusted his hands on the seat of the

old tunic he wore for work; at least he was as tall as Jason. "I thought you were in Antioch by now! Hard luck, your father keeping you hanging around here when you must be keen to be doing something yourself! Are the roads north not safe? Things weren't too bad when I went to Gerasa, but of course that was last summer."

Jason's eyes narrowed, though the smile stayed. He was about to start on a long and clearly amusing account of his own future when his father called him. The relief showed a little too clearly; as they left the yard Eupolemus seemed to be complaining about his son disturbing workmen and Jason's clear voice drifted back, "Oh, that wasn't a proper workman. Didn't you recognize Apollodorus's son? What a come-down!"

Conan hit clumsily with his mallet and struck his thumb. The pain gave his eyes a reason to water.

Towards midday Xenos came out of his room, too restless any longer to try to pretend that he was working. The storeyard was out of the wind and Philo was sitting on a bench against the wall, enjoying the quiet hour before he would have to help serve the tribune's lunch.

"It's going to be hot here as soon as there's any real sun," Philo said. "We shall have to try to fix up some sort of shelter."

"Wasn't there a roll of matting that Conan didn't throw away? Where did he put it?" said Xenos, glad of anything to distract himself. "Isn't it in the covered shed past the stable?"

He went out into the main yard, dodging the horses of the tribune's guard who were being led out for exercise. There seemed to be more people about than usual. He found what he wanted after some poking around. Then he wondered if he could carry it. The roll was half rotten and started to unroll, and his fingers made larger holes than there were already as he tried to grip it tightly. He nearly left it and went for help, but something stubborn inside him wanted to do as simple a thing as this on his own for once. He blundered out into the yard, not able to see properly where he was going, and hoping he would not put his feet in the fresh horse-muck.

It was an angry shout close in front of him that stopped him dead and caused him finally to lose his grip on the matting. It fell in folds over his own feet and those of the man who had shouted, and as he bent to catch hold of the ends he was aware of high-laced army sandals and a red tunic. Even as the voice roared at him again, right into his face and he looked up at the furious Decimus picking straw off his tunic, his mind jarred and seemed to turn as violently in his head as the heart does when it misses a beat.

Decimus was shouting at him, and Philo was suddenly there, trying to brush him down and getting cuffed for his trouble. Xenos murmured something, he did not know what, for this had happened before and he knew where. He turned blindly and stumbled into their room, leaving the matting lying in the courtyard.

Lucia, looking up from her cooking, stared after him in alarm. "What did the centurion say?" she asked Philo. "Xenos seemed so upset!"

"Nothing much, it was just one of his usual bellows. It was mild for him really, because he did look funny with the straw sticking all over him."

He came back an hour later to find Lucia still alone and no sign of Xenos. "Do you think I ought to see if he's all right?" he asked.

Lucia looked doubtfully at the curtained doorway. There had been no sound from inside. "Perhaps he's asleep."

"Then it won't hurt to look."

Philo drew a corner of the curtain aside, trying not to let too much light into the room, but Xenos was not asleep. He was sitting on the bed staring down at his hands, and when the shaft of light moved across the floor he looked up. Philo noticed that although it had not reached his face there seemed something like a glow about it. Then Xenos looked at him, smiled, and spoke gently in a voice that was unlike any that Philo had heard him use before.

"My name is Hylas and my God has found me."

VIII

THE DESTRUCTION AT NOONDAY

PHILO STOOD speechless inside the doorway. The man on the bed got up and came over and embraced him.

"That's good-bye from Xenos," said Hylas, his face still wet from tears. "Thank you for all the care you took of him."

They both sat down, facing each other. Philo said, "You look happy, do you like being who you are? Are you glad you remembered?" It would be awful to remember one was a criminal.

"I don't know what to say. A lot that came back has hurt, but there was so much else—good things that have left my mind empty all these months."

"How did you remember?"

"It was Decimus. When he shouted at me like that it was something that had happened before, or almost the same way. It clicked in my mind, I remembered the other time—and whom it was it happened to."

Outside someone bellowed Philo's name. "Goodness, I'm supposed to be working, and I wanted to hear all of it now!" Philo got up hurriedly.

"A whole lifetime? Actually, if Conan doesn't need his

bed, I'd like to be quiet for a little longer. I have a lot to think about. And it might be simpler to tell you all together."

"Hylas?"

"What?"

"Nothing. I was just practising to see if I'd got it right. It's a nice name, but it doesn't suit you yet. Can I tell Lucia?"

The voice bellowed again. "Yes, but it sounds as if you'll have to be quick about it."

When Philo had let the door curtain fall behind him Hylas, who had been Xenos, was alone in the quiet half-darkness; suddenly tired, he lay down with his hands behind his head. It was strange to be able to look back on his life almost with the detachment of a stranger. He had been right, there had been almost no family, though many friends, and one in particular, the tribune Camillus Rufus whose voice had come to him before the return of the rest of his memories. Had Camillus, probably in Britain by now, heard yet that Hylas had disappeared somewhere in Judaea? Members of the Imperial Secretariat were not supposed to disappear. It was natural that he had remembered Nero so well; had he not worked in his palace in Rome for four years?

He must write to Camillus, but not quite yet, not till he understood better himself what had happened to him, for he saw now behind the actions that had brought him to Judaea a pattern far beyond his own intentions and imagination. He had told Philo that his God had found him, but that had first happened long ago in Rome when he had been a slave. Yes, he remembered all that now, the childhood in a senator's household and how he earned his freedom.

Philo would enjoy that part of the story. Then after his life in Rome there had been a time in Athens in the household of the procurator, growing nearer almost unwillingly to the new purpose that the God who had claimed him had for his life.

He had volunteered to be transferred to the household of the legate of Syria when the Judaean war started, but could it be that he had been needed in Judaea for a reason that even he knew nothing of at the time? Would he be able to explain that to Philo and Conan? Briefly he felt a strong wave of resentment against the God who had brought him to Philadelphia through such suffering and confusion, and yet could he doubt that there had been a purpose behind it and that out of the suffering good had come, both for this family who had sheltered him and on the pass to Macherus? No, through all that had happened he had never been forsaken, and even in the worst of the pain he had not been alone. He did not have to understand more than that at the moment, or decide yet what he should do next. His life had been so full of talking and importance and business that he had never learned to listen. He could learn that here in this small and crowded room as well as anywhere.

He said it out loud, but softly, his voice husky with tears. "I am a follower of the Way. I have a God who has saved me through suffering from anything that evil can do to me. Teach me, Lord, through my own smaller pain how to draw nearer to you and your purpose for me." It was not a proper prayer, but it was so long since he had prayed.

Then there were other words in his mind, part of a Jewish hymn he had sung—where? It was in Athens, not in Rome where he had first believed.

"I will say to the Lord, He is my refuge and my fortress; my God, in him will I trust . . .

I will not be afraid of the terror that comes in the night; nor of the arrow that flieth by day;

Nor for the pestilence that walks in darkness; nor for the destruction that wastes at noonday.

Because he has set his love on me I will deliver him; I will raise him up because he has known my name . . ."

The words came now with the warmth of a blessing, as if spoken by a much loved and completely trusted voice. So much that had happened seemed very long ago and he was tired; Hylas got up to bathe the traces of tears from his face and then lay down again; he slept almost at once and without dreams.

Outside, as the afternoon passed, the house was quiet. Even the Romans seemed to be resting; after all one could not mourn a dead Emperor, and particularly one who had only survived a few months, every hour of the day. Philo, polishing the tribune's mess silver, thought the hours had never dragged so slowly. Xenos whom he had loved had gone, and Hylas, a stranger, was behind the curtain of their room. Xenos had had no previous life and because of that he had belonged to them completely, like a member of the family who shared with them all that he remembered. Philo was afraid that he was going to be very shy of Hylas.

He finished his work at last and went back through the storeyard and behind the fence to Lucia's lean-to where she was lighting the fire to cook their evening meal.

"He hasn't woken yet? I suppose he must be asleep or the curtain wouldn't still be down," he said.

Conan came in behind him. "Who hasn't woken up?"

"Hylas."

"Who on earth is that?" Conan was tired and still upset from the morning's meeting with Jason. He flung himself down on the bench, looking dusty and cross.

As if he had been an actor waiting to make an entrance Hylas drew back the door curtain and came out into the sunny courtyard. For a moment he stood blinking almost shyly, looking across at the suddenly speechless family group.

Then Lucia smiled and held out her hand, shooing Conan to make room for him on the bench

Hylas walked over, took her hand and kissed it, and as he sat down he said, "Greetings from Hylas, son of Pylades, late of the Imperial diplomatic service."

"Oh Hylas, really?" said Philo.

"Yes, I suppose it explains my handwriting. Well, not completely. I was first taught that as a slave."

Conan had turned and was staring at Hylas as if he had never seen him before, all his own weariness and bad temper draining away. He took the man's hand, then he laughed, put his arms round him and gave him a more brotherly hug.

"It's happened? You know . . . ?"

"I know. Steady, Conan, or one of my scars will crack. I've still got those even though I've changed my name."

"Hylas!"

"Yes, Hylas, you were right, I am Greek."

"Now tell us everything, we've waited more than five months," said Philo, squatting down comfortably by Lucia's hearth and looking up at the familiar face that was already different in some way that he could not put into words.

"What can I tell you?" Hylas asked Conan.

"What you would have told us if you had come to us like any ordinary traveller. We have no right to know more than that."

"Very well then. I am Hylas, who was born into the household of the senator Caius Pomponius Afer, the son of his mother's maid and his secretary. My father was called Pylades and he had been born free. I was a bright child, so my master paid to have me trained as a secretary too, and when I was about sixteen I began to work for him. It was more than a year later that he was found dead in his bed one morning with a knife in his side."

"Murdered?" breathed Philo. "Did you see him?"

"Yes, I did, and the blood of a murdered man smells as disgusting as any other blood; it is not something one enjoys seeing. But my master's death nearly caused my own as well, as the whole household was arrested on suspicion, though for the first few days I escaped. No, Philo, I'll tell you that part later!"

Lucia laughed at the sight of Philo's amazed face. "Take no notice, Hylas. But tell me, was your mother still living then?"

"Yes, she was arrested along with the others, if you can imagine what—in Rome—that meant. It did not seem possible that I could do more to help her than give her the consolation of knowing I was still alive. But it was then that I found I had been sent a friend and an unlikely one. There are not many young tribunes who would trouble to concern themselves with the death of slaves, but Camillus Rufus, my master's son-in-law, was fortunately one of them."

Hylas broke off, smiling to himself, remembering Camillus as he had been then, young and very idealistic, making mistakes from sheer enthusiasm; suddenly learning and with some pain that a slave could be as much a man as a senator's son.

"I think he is in Britain now, Camillus. Our lives have brought us together only three or four times, but then, the first time, he saved me. With his help I found the proof that was needed to free the other slaves, and at that very moment I was captured myself. It's strange, it was the memory of that which brought everything back this morning." He put his head back and laughed. "Decimus's face was so like the others's—only I didn't laugh then.

"Please!" begged Philo. "We're letting you go very fast, but you must explain that bit!"

"Very well. It was my own fault. Although I was an escaped slave I found myself in the wrong place one morning in broad daylight, needing to get back to Camillus's house with the last part of my story safe in my mind. I had the bad idea that if I carried something on my head it would act as a disguise and I picked up a sodden, thrown away palliasse. I can still remember the smell. It started coming to pieces at once and fell down over my eyes so that I couldn't see where I was going. When it finally tore in two the straw fell on an officer of the guard outside my master's house. A man who was looking for an escaped secretary. He noticed my writing bump too, Philo."

"Is that when it happened, Hylas? Your back?"

"Yes." Hylas did not go on immediately and no one dared to question him; they had all seen the scars. Then he smiled again. "But we were all freed; Camillus did it. When he was sure of the facts he made the person responsible for the murder confess and went to the Emperor for a free pardon. He freed me and recommended me to a friend in the palace secretariat. That, mostly, has been my life ever since."

"But what were you doing in Judaea?" asked Conan.

"I suppose that started last year when the Emperor was visiting Achaea. I was there too as part of the staff that had to continue the business of the Empire even while Nero sang songs and played at all the Greek games. Before I could return to Rome the Jewish trouble broke out. When things like that happen it isn't only legions that get moved about, civil servants do too. There's a lot of paper work involved in supplying them and arranging the political side of what happens when a country is invaded. The legate sent me on a mission to King Agrippa of Ituraea and then I went down to Judaea."

He paused, looking thoughtfully down at Philo at his feet but hardly seeming to see him.

Conan said quietly, "You don't have to tell us everything. It was a big jump from a king's palace to being a hunted fugitive. I expect it isn't only your story, you can't tell just anyone about it."

Philo thought, 'But we aren't just anyone, we love him.' He wanted to know what had happened more than anything he could remember, but he loved Hylas enough to understand that he must not ask.

Then Hylas looked up again and smiled at their concerned faces. "It's not that I don't trust you, I was wondering if I had the right to tell you something that it might be dangerous for you to know. You see, I am a follower of the Way, the Christos. I had word when I was in the north, in Syria, that there were still Christians in Judaea, caught between the Jews and the Romans. Even after Vespasian drew back from the siege of Jerusalem last summer it was very difficult to get out of the city. The Jews are so divided among themselves, and they fear each other almost as much as Rome. I saw that I had special skills that might be useful, I knew how to make a Roman officer believe me, for example. I had inside knowledge; I thought I could be useful. I never expected to have to help lead a party of refugees through occupied territory. If I had I suppose I should never have gone."

"So that was why the patrol tortured you!" breathed Philo.

"Yes. And now I know why I can begin to accept what happened. You see, I had spent too long with papers and letters and officials and I had forgotten how it felt to be hunted and without hope—I had known it once. When I actually saw the people I had almost carelessly thought I could help, they were strong and brave but this was something beyond their strength. I had to help with the practical things as well. There were women with babies who had been born during the first siege, who had never so much as seen a tree outside the walls, and sick people, and some whose influence and teaching were too precious to lose."

He stopped and smiled again. "Now, I've told you! Lucia, are we going to eat tonight? I missed my lunch, remember!"

The others got up but Philo stayed where he was, deep in his own thoughts, understanding what a precious gift it was that Hylas had given them. Once fate had put him into their hands to save his life, but now of his own choice he had given his future to them again.

IX

THE MAN IN THE ALLEY

PHILO WOKE the next morning with the good feeling that something special had happened, although it was some moments before he could imagine what. Then he remembered Hylas and turned over so that he could look at him, still asleep so close in the other bed. All he could see in the half light was the top of a dark head and an arm thrown out; the rope scars still made a faint bracelet around his wrist. Then he tried to imagine how the room would be without Hylas. He had assured them the evening before that he had no plans yet to leave Philadelphia, indeed he was not yet strong enough to make the journey, but the moment would come one day. Philo pushed the thought to the back of his mind.

That morning the sun had warmth in it for the first time. When the spring rains came the steep streets of Philadelphia would turn into muddy streams and all the shutters would bang, but for the moment the clouds were high. On the surface nothing seemed to have been changed by what had happened. Conan went out to the stoneyard, Lucia was sitting mending a tunic and Hylas had pulled his table near the door and continued with his copying; only Philo felt different.

Fulvius the mess steward, who saw to the main running of the house, noticed Philo's good spirits and realized that he was likely to prove a nuisance indoors and not to be trusted with the unpacking of the new table-ware. He was a Syrian, even darker than the tribune, a small wiry man with a passion for fixing things. He was equally good at mending a couch leg and at finding figs in the city when there were none to be had. At first Philo had been uncertain whether he could trust him, for Fulvius had been exasperated by the boy's clumsiness, but after he saw that Philo was at least willing, they got on better.

"Spices!" said Fulvius. "You of anyone ought to know where we can best get those, and I'm told there is no saffron left in the city. See what you can do, only don't pay a silly price. No need to hurry yourself."

Philo gave him a grateful look and was out of sight before Fulvius could think of further errands that might have meant carrying back a heavy basket.

He knew just where to go, not to the stalls in the market square but to the warehouse of Paulinus. If there was any saffron to be had Gorion the scribe would know where it was.

It was a long time since he had pushed down the narrow alley past donkeys waiting to be unloaded and dark muleboys speaking all the dialects from Arabia to Antioch. He had been keeping away from the part of the city that reminded him of his father. Today he felt different, ready to be back in this small world of smells and colours and gossip about people and prices.

Gorion was an elderly Jew, one of the few still working in the city who had survived the riots. He worked as a clerk in Paulinus's warehouse, and Philo hoped that it would be possible to talk to him without meeting the merchant. He was never likely to forgive Paulinus for the way he had spoken in the market square on the morning when news of Apollodorus's death had reached Philadelphia. If it meant waiting for a good moment he was not in a hurry, there was so much to see.

He had been standing for some time in a convenient corner where he would not be bumped by the donkeys passing with loads that almost filled the narrow alley, when he had the feeling that he was being watched. In all that crowd and noise it seemed fanciful, but Philo turned all the same to peer under the dim archways further up the hill. It seemed to him that a dark young man drew back at that moment into a doorway. Philo saw only the back of his head and the set of his shoulders, but there was something familiar about him.

He turned away, pretending to have noticed nothing, and then glanced back quickly. The man was still there, and this time, despite an unfamiliar beard, Philo knew him. Nicanor had not changed that much.

Without stopping to think that his brother might not want to be recognized Philo ran down the alley. Nicanor seemed to hesitate and before he had time to disappear Philo had him by the arm.

"Not here!" hissed Nicanor, seeing the tears in his brother's eyes and the probability of a noisy and conspicuous greeting. He pulled Philo back through the doorway and into the dim spaces of a warehouse stacked with bundles of hides. It was dark and the smell was terrible, but suddenly quiet after the racket of the alley outside.

Philo held on to his brother by both arms and looked up at him. Of course he had known Nicanor, but now he was wondering how. The beard was young and silky, not much more than a beginning, but the hair had grown shaggy and the eyes seemed more deeply set; the lines round the mouth were different too.

"Why haven't you been back?" There seemed to be no place for the normal greetings and exchange of news.

"Did you really expect me? With them in the house?"

"But Lucia . . ."

"I know, you aren't the only one who loves her. If I ever came it would be to see her. I suppose I will some day, but not yet. Don't look like that, Philo, I'm glad to see you—but not Conan, the Romans were his idea."

"Not really, it was me, and Hylas too."

"Who's Hylas?" The strange name brought a flicker of interest to the dark preoccupied eyes.

Philo explained. Nicanor leant back against a pile of bales, his face almost hidden in the gloom. When Philo finished there was a moment's silence, then when he spoke again Nicanor's voice was different, not so defensive.

"Then I suppose he'd understand. I wish I'd known, it would have been a help. Now listen, I haven't got long, Cousin Chares is expecting me back at the farm before midday. Yes, I'm still there, but not for much longer, though he doesn't know that. One day he'll come puffing into the city to find out where I've gone and you're not to tell him what I'm going to tell you now. Do you understand?"

Philo nodded uncomprehendingly.

"It's like this. I've had time since I left home to sort things out in my own mind. I don't think I quite knew what I was doing when I went off; I do now. You know what Lucia told us about being a Jew, the way it comes from the mother? I've thought a lot about that, because I came to see that if it was true I didn't have to stay in Philadelphia and be my father's son and keep out of trouble with the Romans. I know how Father saw things, but he's dead and I'm alive and things have changed. There are still Jews in this city, you know that; I went to them. There's more, far more to it than I ever imagined, and the time's far too short to learn properly. But any time now the war will start again and I know it's my war and I want to be part of it—and I know on which side."

"But you aren't a Jew, you can't be," wailed Philo in horror.

Nicanor shook him to make him quiet. "In what matters, I am. I've been accepted, I go south any day."

"But you haven't been circumcised!"

"No?"

Philo backed away, and winced instinctively. With pain and dismay he knew now, finally, that Nicanor meant what he said. It was as if he was no longer his brother, but some unfamiliar Jewish Zealot.

"South? Where are you going? Not to Jerusalem?"

"No, Macherus. There's still some hope of holding out there, of saving something. They can't kill us all!"

Could they not? Philo remembered his own tribune, Marius Gallienus, easy-going enough mostly, but at the bottom tough as steel. It sounded as if Nicanor was trying to persuade himself.

"Did Gorion help you in all this?" he asked, suddenly suspicious.

"No, I tried him first, but he would have nothing to do with it. I don't know why. Oh Philo, I am glad I saw you, but it does make things even more difficult!"

Philo wanted to take his brother's hand and go out into the sunshine together on some errand for their father as they had when they were small, with home there to come back to and the next day just the same. But Father was dead and they would never walk up the hill from the market and in at the front gate together again.

He took a step back from his brother. "I could hate you, Nicanor, because we were unhappy enough and now you've made things worse, but I won't. You're hating and I don't think it helps at all. Hylas doesn't and he has even more reason to than you have. Look what the Romans have done to him, and all they did to you was kill a horse! And yet he can live quietly in the same house as the Romans, and I must too. I won't hate people I don't even know and understand. Later I may, but for the moment no."

"Philo, you're only being childish. I'm a man now, things are different for me. Look, I can't bear this, I've got to go."

"Nico, don't forget us. You've changed yourself, you've thrown away everything, we'll still be here, we won't forget you."

Nicanor took his brother by the shoulders with hands that trembled, kissed him quickly and ran out through the doorway. Philo stayed where he was for some time, remembering the unfamiliar touch of his brother's beard, the hard man's hands; then he went quietly out into the alley, found Gorion and did the errand he had been sent to do.

When he had finished he did not go straight home. It seemed days since he left the house so happily, but it was still only mid-morning. Somehow he could not face the direct way home from the market. Without really thinking about it he found himself in the square by the temple. He paused, half wanting to go to his usual watch place on the city wall, to try to sort out the turmoil in his mind, but he had not been there since his father's death. Instead he went through the gate into the stone mason's yard in search of

Conan; he would have to hear about Nicanor some time and it might be easier at once, and away from the house.

Conan could see from his brother's face that something serious had happened; he took Philo out of sight behind a stack of unshaped stone and listened quietly to all he had to say. When it was over he stood looking down at his own dusty hands with the grazes and cuts from the stone-worker's tools.

"Well, at least Nicanor has decided something, and gone through with it. That's more than I have," he said quietly. "And you've got a job too!"

"What could you have done? Not something like that!" And Philo was beginning to wonder about his own work; it was not likely to last very long as things were now.

"Perhaps not, but I can't stay here. It's no good, I like the carving but not here, not in Philadelphia. It's too small, there's Jason . . . Oh, just too much to remind me. Go home now, Philo, try not to worry, there's nothing you, anyway, can do about all this." Suddenly he gave his brother a quick hug. "Thank the Gods for someone who doesn't change!"

Philo was so surprised that he left the yard speechless. It seemed better to tell Lucia nothing of what happened. In the last months she had aged a great deal and she was often in pain with her stiff knees. That night they told Hylas, but there was nothing left that anyone could do except wait.

It was on one of the first really wet days towards the end of the month, when Conan had not gone up to the stone-yard, that he had a talk with Fulvius. He had wandered across to the stables, trying to keep out of Hylas's way in the cramped room, and the steward found him there.

"Well, it won't be long now!" he said. "I understand

Sosthenes will be in the city any day as soon as the road's passable, and then you'll be off. Those biceps are strong enough to carry a shield."

"What shield?" Conan was at a loss.

"Why, I took it for granted that was all you were waiting for! What else can you do? You can't sit around here all your life! Enlist, of course. Where else can you be sure of a job with a pension at the end?"

Conan almost laughed but managed to turn it into an expression of amazement. "In the legion? But I'm not a citizen!"

"Did I say the legion, though there are worse places to be? What about the auxiliaries? Vespasian started the war with at least twenty thousand. Sosthenes will be recruiting for the Foot Auxiliaries. It's not a bad life, twenty-five years' service and then the citizenship as a bonus!"

"Twenty-five years!" said Conan. The whole idea was absurd. If he lived that long he would be over forty.

Fulvius cocked an eyebrow at him and understood very well what was going on in the boy's head. He had only said what seemed obvious; he had nothing to gain by pushing Conan except another chance of proving his reputation as one who saw further than most.

Hylas noticed the preoccupied look, wondered what was on his mind and decided not to ask. Conan would tell him later; there was no one else he could talk to about things that would have worried Lucia and perplexed Philo. The younger boy was growing up quickly but he had his own problems.

That, unfortunately, was the night when Marius Gallienus struck Philo, and not without some justification. Officers from the fifth legion were passing through and the tribune was only too glad of the chance for a party. Fulvius had ordered something special and the guests had put on their best tunics.

For Philo the evening started badly. A chilly wind was blowing down from the citadel into the courtyard, so that as the servants hurried backwards and forwards their hands were alternately hot and cold. That was why Philo dropped the cup, one of the best ones. Fulvius cuffed him—not very hard—and said he would sort it out in the morning, but the boy was already tense and frightened when he began to wait at table. Somehow the room seemed even noisier than usual, and the smell of wine stronger. Gallienus never got more than flushed when he drank, but not all the visitors were so lucky.

Suddenly Philo hated them, hated Rome and the Emperor and the endless war that in its own way had reached out and harmed his family; all that Nicanor had said seemed true. Most of all he hated standing in a blue tunic filling drinking cups and mopping up greasy tables. He wished he was out of it all with Nicanor, out of sound of all Romans.

Then one of the visitors, a fat young man, called for a damp towel to wipe his sweating face. Sunk in misery, Philo did not hear him the first time; at the second shout he shied like a startled horse and bumped into the table by the tribune's couch. The wine from his cup slopped over and splashed the breast of his white tunic.

"Idiot!" said the tribune. "Come here."

It was only three steps, but all the strangers were jeering by now. Gallienus's eyes were very bright; he slapped Philo hard across the face and said, "Now get out!"

The laughter followed him into the cold courtyard. As he stumbled over the steps, eyes blinded by tears, a hand caught his shoulder. "Go to the kitchen, wait there." It was Fulvius, using the sort of voice one did not disobey.

Without it Philo would have gone straight over the back wall without a cloak and run till he was lost, as Fulvius well knew. As it was he spent the next hour huddled on a stool in the corner of the kitchen, trying to keep from under the cook's feet and hoping he would have died before Fulvius came and punished him again. He had never felt so helpless in his life.

It was very late when Fulvius did come. Philo got up, clumsy with exhaustion, and stood, a hand to his bruised cheek. Fulvius turned him towards the lamp.

"Hm, that will show by morning. I don't think we're going to make a dining-room servant of you, so we shall have to think of something else. No, don't look like that. Didn't you see the tribune was only trying to get you out of harm's way before that fat idiot started to make fun of you? If our Marius had been in earnest you'd have lost your front teeth. Now, go to bed and we'll sort it out in the morning."

Philo started to go and then turned back irresolute, nearer to tears now that Fulvius had been kind, and not yet able to believe that this was all that was going to happen.

"What's the matter? Oh, I see. Don't imagine anyone's going to waste a good flogging on you tomorrow, we've got better ways of wearing ourselves out. Now do as you're told and go to sleep."

Philo went. As he slid down in the bed Conan grunted in protest at the cold air and then laid an arm across his chest. Then the room was quiet again, but it was much later before Philo slept.

X

GORION THE SCRIBE

PHILO'S STOMACH woke him very early in the morning with the uncomfortable cramps that begin a day when something frightening is going to happen. He shot out of bed and made for the latrine, and when he came back later feeling empty and chilly Hylas was awake.

"What's the matter? Have you been sick?" he asked in a whisper, not to wake Conan.

"Not exactly. I'm better now." It was still nearly an hour before he needed to get up. He slid into bed carefully beside his brother. Conan grunted and turned over to face the wall. Something in Philo's voice caught Hylas's attention; he sat up and looked at him, and even in the half light he could see the boy's bruised cheek.

"What's that?"

Philo told him from the beginning. "And Fulvius is right, I hate it, working in the dining-room, and I'm clumsy. But what am I going to do? I'm not very clever with my hands, and now we can't afford school any more how am I ever going to learn to earn my living?"

"Hm," said Hylas, "I rather wondered how that was going to work out. A Roman mess isn't the best place for a boy of good family to work in; I remember only too well what it was like when I was your age. But let's be practical, there has to be something you're good at. You looked after me very well when I was hurt."

That pleased Philo but seemed to lead nowhere.

"Wait a minute," said Hylas suddenly, "I've thought of something."

"What?"

"Who was the old Jew who came to the back gate not long ago? You went out to talk to him; the one with grey side curls."

"Old Gorion, Paulinus's clerk?"

"Is that his name? Why did he come?"

"He always had a great respect for Father and he came to see how we were. Why do you want to know?"

"You were talking to him nineteen to the dozen. What language was it?"

"Aramaic, of course. He speaks Greek but his Aramaic is more fun. Father taught me and I was practising. Hebrew is the formal Jewish language of their scriptures but Aramaic is what they actually speak and write."

"You sounded pretty fluent. What other languages do you speak besides Greek?"

"Latin of course, ugly language! And enough Syrian for shopping, and some of the dialect the Arabs use—it's very like Aramaic. Why?"

"You pick up languages easily."

"I suppose I do. Father used to joke about it and say how useful it would be on my first journey." Philo stopped suddenly, back on forbidden ground where he could not trust himself. That was the golden future that had rolled up suddenly in his face like a closed scroll. It only hurt to remember it.

Hylas noticed but pretended not to. "Which of those languages can you write?" he asked.

"Greek and Latin."

"Not Aramaic?"

"I know a few of the letters, Gorion started to teach me once."

"I wonder if that could be the answer. Here across Jordan and in Judaea the army is going to need secretaries and clerks who can understand what Jewish prisoners are saying and read Aramaic documents. It's an awkward language and the Romans aren't quick to understand strange alphabets. The main thing when you have to earn your living is to find a skill that someone else hasn't got and that they'll pay you for. What do you think?"

That would mean being drawn even more closely into the war, the terrible war that had already divided Nicanor from his family. For a moment Philo felt that he could not bear it, that good as this idea was he wanted no more to do with the Romans, let alone to work even more closely with them. But what else was there? He pushed the doubts away and tried to look at Hylas's plan from the practical point of view.

"Gorion would teach me properly, I know he would. But what would Fulvius think?"

It was almost day now and the house was beginning to stir. Philo sat up and saw that Hylas was smiling.

"I think Fulvius would be rather relieved, and, do you know, I think Gorion might find himself with two pupils. I would like to learn Aramaic myself!"

"Why?"

"I'll tell you later if it works out."

"I'm not sure I can explain all this to Fulvius."

"It sounds as if I'd better. It would come more easily from me," said Conan.

"How long have you been awake?" asked Philo in surprise, getting up and feeling for his sandals.

"Not all that long." Conan sat up. "Hylas, do you think it would work?"

Hylas said, "It has a right feel about it. If Philo is prepared to work harder and quicker at something difficult than he ever has before, I think he may find that a bruised face has been worth it."

It seemed almost at once that Hylas's "feel" had been right, for as soon as he reached his office that morning Marius Gallienus sent for Philo, and Conan followed him uninvited into the room.

The tribune raised an eyebrow. "Council for the defence?" he asked.

"Rather more a witness, sir, if you will allow me," said Conan, who had always found the young Roman easy to talk to.

"Very well. Now, boy, let's have a look at you." He came round to the other side of his table and turned Philo's head towards the light with one strong hand.

"You know you deserved that and rather more?" Philo nodded, suddenly very scared that Fulvius had been wrong about the flogging.

"So what are we going to do with you?"

"You haven't got a use for a clerk with a knowledge of Aramaic, have you?" asked Conan.

"Are you asking me for a job?"

"Not for me, for Philo."

"He writes Aramaic?"

"Not quite, but he speaks it well and he could be writing in a couple of months."

The tribune was used to making up his mind fast. "You've got one month to prove it. Meanwhile half pay and your meals, and any odd jobs Fulvius can find, but not in the dining-room. Now clear out and let me get on."

Fulvius saw them go and then went into the tribune's room; he found him well pleased with what had happened.

"I thought Philo would come up with something, he's an inventive sort of boy. I wonder about the older brother though. Do you think he'd make a soldier?"

Gallienus sat back in his chair. "Conan? I hadn't thought about it. As an auxiliary of course. He's about the age and reasonably well built. Finding a good Aramaic secretary would be worth an introduction to Agrippa's Auxiliary Commander. I don't see that there's anything else Conan can do, and he's a good enough lad. Things haven't been easy for him, being the eldest."

He went through the doorway and up the steps to the storeyard. Pausing at the stable door he looked across at the small courtyard where Conan was talking to Lucia, seeing him for the first time in a different light. In uniform and a helmet he would look a man; the boyish good looks would be fading soon away.

As soon as he had told Hylas what had happened Philo went down to the market again. Now he was half looking out for Nicanor, although it was unlikely that he would be in the city two days running. It was not easy to go down the same narrow alley, at the rear of Paulinus's warehouse. He found Gorion where he had expected, checking the pannier loads of a train of donkeys. Philo curled himself round a corner to wait for a chance to speak to him. Gorion noticed him quickly and made a wait-and-see gesture. It was an hour before the last of the sacks were counted and he folded his tablets with a snap and shuffled off towards a stall which was selling fresh bread rings. In a corner where two walls met, out of the wind, Philo was waiting for him.

"You wanted me again, young master? How can I serve you?"

His politeness hurt; Philo suddenly realized that he had not worked out with Hylas how he was going to pay for the lessons.

"I don't know how to ask you," he said, suddenly shy of the old man he had known all his life, and starting to stammer.

The seamed face smiled. Gorion cracked the fresh seed-sprinkled bread ring he was holding and gave Philo half. "Eat and talk, son of my old friend. Boys are always hungry."

Philo started to chew automatically, but suddenly he felt better. "Do you remember trying to teach me the Aramaic alphabet once?"

"Indeed I do. You would have learned it quickly if you had persevered."

"Could you teach me again?"

"Surely."

"But, Gorion, I can't pay you for lessons, not at first, and this time there would be two of us."

"Have I asked for money? But who is this other pupil—not your brother?"

"Conan? Oh no, it's . . ." How did one explain Hylas.

"I see, I think I see. I should come to your house quietly to the back gate, and we can talk in comfort and see if your mind is still quick. Tonight I'm not sure, but I may be free. You will be there?"

"Yes, Gorion. Any night you can come. It's . . . if I can write Aramaic perhaps I can find work."

"And with that will come respect again. For such a reason every night I will come. Now, I have my own job to keep."

The old man turned and threaded his way between the market stalls.

That afternoon Hylas rested from his copying work, saving his eyes for the evening, and the hope of their first lesson. Philo came into the room in the late afternoon to light the lamp and found Hylas lying back with his eyes shut but a faint smile on his mouth.

"What are you thinking about? You look happy."

"I was enjoying the feeling of having made a plan that seemed to be the right one. That, and the thought of the Aramaic itself."

"Why do you want to learn it so much? You said you'd tell me."

Hylas opened his eyes and sat up. "Because it is the language that my Lord spoke to his friends. I want to have the sound of it in my own mouth, to be able to read what he read."

"Your Lord? Your former master, do you mean?" Philo was completely lost. It did not sound at all like the murdered senator or anyone else he had heard about so far.

Hylas laughed, "Not my master, my Lord—the God I serve. The Christos." He used the Greek word.

Then Philo understood, and with the knowledge came fear and concern and great affection.

"When you told us that first time that you were a Christian I don't think I really understood. But Hylas, the Emperor . . . in Rome they've killed the followers of Christos!"

"And not only in Rome. I have friends who have died in Bithynia and Syria. Have I frightened you, Philo? You know I would never bring danger on you here. I would leave at once; but I've been careful."

"It isn't that, and you know we don't want you to go."

"Nor do I, yet. I think I have a little more time here. Listen, isn't that someone outside?"

It was almost dark now in the yard, but from the doorway Philo saw the bent figure of Gorion talking to his brother by the light of the lamp at the back gate. He went out to welcome him and to bring him in.

Gorion looked at the young man with the scarred face. "Yes, the stranger, the burnt man from the desert. I thought it would be you."

They greeted each other courteously, and then Hylas said, "It's a long time since I was brought in. I hoped people had forgotten me."

"Oh yes, almost. There have been so many dying and dead men since last summer. You're safe enough here, in the very house of the Roman commander, and your secret is safe, from those who should not know it. But I hear some things my master doesn't, and I and my friends have not forgotten the man who saved the followers of the Way who had escaped from Jerusalem. How could we?"

It was very still in the small room, so that Philo found himself listening to his own breathing. Hylas suddenly seemed a long way away, though his eyes were still open and Gorion was watching him with the eye of a fisherman who has cast his line in what he hopes is the right place.

"Even here? And all these months I haven't known and I thought myself alone on this side of the river. I should have trusted more! So you understand what learning Aramaic would mean to me?"

"You want to hear his voice in the words? Is it not a blessing in my own life?"

He took the young man's hands in his. Philo suddenly had a feeling that he was very much in the way in the small room, and Hylas as usual sensed his feeling almost before he knew it himself.

"Poor Philo, I think we shall have to leave the first lesson till tomorrow. Gorion and I have much to discuss, but perhaps he can leave us the alphabet to learn."

As Philo went out of the room he wondered if he was jealous of Gorion. But how could he feel like that about anyone who could bring such a light into Hylas's face? He knew him so much better now than he had when they had fought for his life on the first day after he was brought into the house; it stirred him deeply to understand that his friend was still in danger in a new and more difficult way. The sound of loud Roman laughter, so close through the archway, made him shiver as he went to say good night to Lucia and invent a soothing story of why the lessons had not begun.

XI

AUXILIARY RECRUIT

CONAN STOOD stiffly to attention in front of the table in Gallienus's room while an elegant young Syrian in a dark red cloak looked at him from different angles. Outside the spring rain poured down in the courtyard, splashing from the eaves of the colonnade. Conan had taken three days to think about what Fulvius had said, and now he could see that there had never really been a chance of his deciding any other way. It only remained for Sosthenes, the young Herodian commander of Sosthenes' Foot Auxiliaries, to see it the same way.

"Well, he looks fit enough, tribune. He can read and write and he hasn't got a criminal record. I can't be choosey these days. A pity he can't afford a horse. The third company's under strength and I don't know where I'm going to get mounts from. Not from the Arabians at their prices."

"I'm afraid there's no question of a horse," said Gallienus. "Conan will have to foot-slog like a lot of good men before him. When does the draft start north for Caesarea?"

"The day after tomorrow, if I can round them all up by then. This season's recruits are a rough lot and I shall be hard pressed to get them even partly trained by the time Vespasian's ready. If he ever is." He turned back to Conan.

"So there it is. Report to the barracks tomorrow evening. You'll march north at dawn two days from now and as I don't intend to have twenty crying sets of relations to deal with then, I want you in the night before. Get the farewells over tomorrow."

"Yes, sir." Conan didn't know how to salute so he bowed instead and tried to get out of the room tidily, feeling two pairs of amused eyes on his back.

He found a place on the far side of the courtyard where he could watch the door of the tribune's office. He felt as cold and heavy inside as if his stomach were full of grey porridge, and he could still feel how Sosthenes had touched him, feeling his muscles as if he had been a slave in the market. But he might have been just that so easily; at least he had chosen this.

Voices sounded louder across the courtyard, Sosthenes was leaving. The two men came out from under the arch. "Is it still raining? No, not so much, Jupiter be praised. Another day like today and the roads north would have been washed away for good. Orderly, my horse!"

When Gallienus came back from seeing his visitor off he found Conan loitering uncomfortably outside his door.

"Not having second thoughts?" he asked, suddenly seeing the boy as he was now and as he would be when the army had put its mark upon him.

"No, sir, it was just that I wanted to thank you. I know some companies are better than others, and it makes a difference. Sosthenes might not have taken me without your word."

"Possibly not. Now it's up to you." He turned to go into his room but then paused again. "You've probably had all the advice you can manage from Fulvius, most of it good. One last word from me. It's quicker to learn something the first time—don't argue, and do as you're told. You can work out if you were told right later, when you've more experience."

Suddenly Conan wished he was leaving at once. The long hours of the next day were going to be almost more than he could bear to live through and now Lucia must be told. The tribune was right, it was easier to do things quickly.

Lucia knew, of course. Conan had never needed before to try to conceal his plans, and he had not been particularly good at it. Philo helped his brother to pack his things almost in silence, Lucia made a pitiful attempt at a special farewell meal, and then the last hours were mercifully over.

There had been no more rain and the second dawn was cold and clear. For the first time in his life Conan was woken by trumpets; he picked himself up, his eyes still half closed with sleep, and began to roll up the blanket he had been sleeping in. The floor had been hard and damp and there had been bugs. As the decurion in charge of the detail of recruits roared at them from the doorway he could not imagine how he was going to march twenty miles that day.

The squad was lined up in the barrack square outside, a strange assortment, shivering in the half-light. Conan bent to retie his sandal thong but jerked upright as he was roared at again.

To his surprise Sosthenes himself came to see them go. The decurion saluted so smartly Conan thought his backbone would snap.

"All correct, Terentius? No defaulters?"

"Only one, sir, and I was never sure of him."

"Right, thirty-five recruits to deliver. Six days to Caesarea, do you think?"

"It depends on the roads, sir, and they're a raw lot."

"Very well, decurion, we shan't expect any records. March off."

There were few people about so early in the market as the raw lot marched through, and no one Conan knew. He was relieved at that; it would be talked about but he wouldn't be there to hear. Better to forget about Philadelphia for the moment, to think only of the long days ahead and putting one foot in front of the other. Then at the northern gate a familiar shape detached itself from the wall: Philo in a dark cloak, his face looking suddenly thinner and older. Their eyes met and Philo raised a hand in greeting; Conan tried to grin but it did not feel as if he had succeeded. Then the arch was dark overhead and the road ran on in the narrow bottom of the valley between the higher hills around the city. Chares's farm was not far away.

The sun was not yet up over the eastern hills and the streets of Philadelphia were still grey as Philo turned from the northern gate and made his way home. His father was gone, Nicanor too, and now with Conan marching northward and away from them for ever the pain of the last long months came to him as freshly as if it were still the first day in the market-place.

He was crying before he knew it, snivelling like a small boy; he turned against the wall of the house he was passing and buried his head in the crook of his arm.

A passing labourer on his way down to the market stopped beside him. "Are you all right, son?"

Philo sniffed hard and wiped his nose on his cloak. "Yes, I fell and banged my elbow and it made my eyes run."

The man seemed satisfied and went off down the hill. Philo wiped his eyes too and went on. Conan had gone and that was that, and twenty-five years was not a lifetime even if it seemed like that at the moment. What else could his brother have done anyway, a tall well-grown boy? That was what armies were for. And he himself wasn't alone, not as Conan would be; there was Hylas. He tried for a moment to imagine how life would be if his father had never found Hylas; it was hardly possible and he blessed the unknown God who filled his friend's life so completely and who had brought him to Philadelphia. It was not the practical things he could do that were such a comfort, but what he was and the ideas he had. What other fugitive from Rome would have thought of bringing Romans into the house? And yet if he had not Philo would not now be coming home to even the remnant of a family.

The eastern edge of the roofs above him turned a fuzzy gold and the street ahead was suddenly full of light. There was warmth in the sun and it looked from the few clouds as if it was not going to rain today. Good for Conan on the road—though he must try not to think so much of Conan—and good for them all, particularly poor Lucia trying to coax her fire to burn. He turned up the steep slope behind the house and went in at the back gate.

Sure enough Lucia was trying to get the fire to go, crimson in the face, with a strand of hair in her eyes. The woodpile looked low. Philo brought over an armful before squatting down beside her on the cracked paving stones.

"He's gone? You saw him?"

"For a minute. He looked a lot older already."

"Well, he would." Lucia said no more about the boy who was the oldest of her nurslings, the child she had cared for since the day he was born. She got painfully to her feet and greeted Hylas as he came out into the sunshine. "Fulvius gave me some almost fresh rolls, could you eat one? It's warm enough to sit out this morning."

She had them ready on a plate covered with a cloth. Philo sat down on the bench beside Hylas with the food between them, and they had breakfast together.

"I sent Gorion away yesterday evening when you were with Conan," said Hylas. "It was no time for an Aramaic lesson, but he left some work for you to translate. He said he might come up later this morning; Paulinus is ill, so he's not as hard pressed as usual."

Somehow Philo supposed he must bring his mind back to his studies, knowing how soon he would have to prove himself to Marius Gallienus. He had learned quickly, knowing that he must, but would the tribune be satisfied with him?

He followed Hylas into their room. The copying-table was already set up but the room seemed larger now, for Lucia had already packed away Conan's things. He could hear her outside washing the bed cover; it seemed a very final thing to do. Philo curled his legs up on the bed that was now his alone and opened his tablets.

Two days later Cousin Chares came, just as Nicanor had foretold, with a letter addressed to Philo. He sat on the bench red-faced and furious at being sent on an errand to a schoolboy, while Lucia fussed over him and Philo tried to explain that the letter was to him because Conan was no longer there. It was not true but seemed the best way out. That set Chares off again.

"Your own cousin! The boy takes a step like that without a word to anyone! Did he consult your uncle?"

Philo was silent, for that had not occurred to any of

them. The fact that he was not the only one to be left out seemed to pacify the farmer. "Well, here's your letter, you'd better read it, I suppose."

Philo broke the seal, suddenly remembering the day he had told Hylas that he had never had a letter. This was one he had never wanted.

"To Philo, son of Apollodorus, greetings. I hope that the God I follow will grant that some day I may see you again although I do not know when that may be. I am going to Macherus where brave men are still resisting Rome. My greetings to Lucia. If you can, think well of me. Farewell!"

"But what's the boy talking about?" asked Chares. "Macherus? What business has he got there? All I know is that when I went to wake him this morning his bed hadn't been slept in. Fine gratitude!"

It was an hour before they had calmed him, with death all the while in their hearts. Only after the puzzled man had left could they speak freely.

"Philo, you knew of this?" There was a deep look of hurt in Lucia's eyes.

He nodded his head. "But I hoped he wouldn't do it, that it was only talk."

"Your brother was not one just to talk, from what I saw of him," said Hylas. "But I doubt if he has any idea yet of what he has done. You've never seen Macherus. It's a bitter place, a palace inside a fortress on a spike of rock, with the town huddled beneath it. The gorge is so deep on three sides that there's only one road in. It squats there with its gate towards the desert and a glimpse across the ravines of the Salt Sea and Judaea beyond. I wonder if any of my friends are still there, I hope not. They would see the smoke when Jerusalem burns." Hylas's voice was full of pain.

"Conan to the north and Nicanor to the south, all in three days," said Lucia. "Thank the Gods my little mistress never lived to see it."

There seemed nothing more to be said.

It was at the beginning of the next month that the tribune called Philo to his office. Decimus was standing by the table, looking at the scroll in his hands with an air of deep frustration.

"Can you make anything of that?" asked Gallienus, taking it from the centurion and tossing it to the boy.

Philo's mouth went dry and he nearly dropped it; this was going to be the moment. But when he unrolled it he almost grinned with relief, only it would not do to admit how easy it was going to be.

"It's mostly names and a list of stores."

"You can translate it all?" asked the tribune.

"Yes, sir."

"Then sit down over there and get on with it."

Philo went over to the clerk's table in the corner of the room. There were writing materials lying there, he weighted down the scroll and pulled the tablets towards him. Then something struck him."

"Greek or Latin, sir?"

"Latin of course," said the centurion crossly, looking at him with suspicion.

That made it a little more difficult; he had to go through an extra stage, because he could not yet think in Latin. He wrote the names down carefully and then the instructions about the collection of stores that made up the second part of the message. Hylas had done wonders for his handwriting. The two officers were still talking; Gallienus was watching the boy unobtrusively but Philo did not notice him as he concentrated on the work before him.

"You've finished? That was quick, let me see," he said, as Philo sat back to check what he had written. The tribune picked up the tablets and studied them while the boy watched his face apprehensively; the Roman seemed pleased.

"Yes, that's clear enough, so long as it's accurate, and we can check that later. Look, Decimus, I told you so, see here."

Both men bent over the tablets in the doorway where the light was good. "Jochanon of Gischala, sir," said the centurion, pointing to a name at the top of the list with a stubby finger.

Gallienus turned back to Philo, who was waiting by his stool wondering if it was Hylas's Jochanon. "Good," he said, looking down at the boy. "That seems just what I wanted. Now I think we'll post the regular man to other duties for a while and see if you can manage the rest of the work, and me! His spelling was vile anyway. Go and ask Fulvius for his stores requisitions and copy it out neatly, and then I shall have two letters for you to write. You know how to write letters properly?"

"I think so," said Philo, trying to remember all Hylas had taught him.

"I hope so for your sake. I can't be bothered with the pompous bits at the beginning and end, I shall leave them to you," said the tribune, trying to look fierce. But Philo was used by now to his size, and the dark face with the large features. Gallienus was one of the strongest-looking men he had ever seen; five years before he must have been a formidable athlete, but his wound and boredom and bad luck had already softened him a little.

Hylas was waiting apprehensively for him on the bench in their courtyard when the tribune finally let him go. "He was pleased; he must have been or he wouldn't have kept you so long."

It was good to be praised, to have Lucia smile and see the satisfaction in Hylas's eyes. Philo held out his hand. "Look, ink! Your mark!"

Within a couple of months Philo could hardly remember when he had not worked in the corner of the square, white-washed room, sunny now in the late spring, copying lists, writing records and listening with half an ear to what the tribune was doing so that he could anticipate the occasional roars when something was wanted fast. He was not often overworked and from time to time the tribune still sent him on errands.

It was late one afternoon when he was coming back across the little square outside the temple; he had been delivering the answer to an invitation from Eupolemus. As he passed the temple steps a young man leaning against the base of a statue spoke his name. He had a dark beard and wildly curling hair, his face was tanned and his clothes a mass of tatters as if he came from the desert. The voice was husky, unfamiliar, but then the man said his name again, and after it his pet name, a word no one outside the family knew. It was something that had happened before.

Philo stopped, trembling, the man moved farther into an angle in the wall, out of sight of passers-by; only the leprous beggar above on the steps was singing his usual tuneless song. Philo looked at the man and then took his outstretched hands.

"Nicanor?"

"How many dark-haired brothers have you? No, idiot, don't hug me, my captain would kill me if he knew I was here, but with luck he never will. Leave the gate unbarred tonight if you can, otherwise I'll come over the wall."

He broke away down a side alley and was out of sight almost at once. Philo went straight home. There was no one in the courtyard and he was able to get to Hylas's room without anyone seeing him, which was as well because he knew that he could not control his face yet.

Hylas took one look, put down his pen and said, "What is it? Not Conan?"

"No, Nicanor, here in the city; he's coming tonight. Should I tell Lucia?"

"How did he look?"

"Like a Jewish outlaw."

"Then no, not till he's here. He may be picked up by a patrol and not come, and then it would be all for nothing."

Philo thought that the last glow would never go from the sky. He waited in the shadows near the gate, seeing the lights in the other courtyard and Fulvius serving dinner. He did not hear footsteps outside in the road, but the door moved gently against its hinges. Philo slipped the bolt quickly and Nicanor came in. It was dark by the gate; he froze still against it while a servant with a loaded dish passed through the lighted patch between the kitchen and the dining-room and then crossed the main storeyard like a shadow.

"I haven't told Lucia, let me go first," said Philo.

He lifted the curtain and went into the old woman's room. She was looking well that night, her legs were giving her less pain and her eyes seemed brighter.

"What is it, Philo?" she said. Then she saw his face and her hands went to her heart.

"No, Lucia, good news. Look!" He held back the curtain and Nicanor came into the room.

Hylas, who had been sitting beside Lucia's bed, stood up quickly and moved back; then Nicanor crossed the room in two paces, knelt down and put his head in the old woman's lap. It was the first gentle thing that Philo had seen his brother do for so long that he felt tears prick behind his eyes. There had been food left over from the evening meal, he had made sure of that; he went out quickly to fetch it and when he came back Nicanor was sitting on the bed beside Lucia, holding her hand. He ate quickly, as if he had not seen food for a long time, and then looked up at their expectant faces. Suddenly he stopped being a strange wild rebel in dirty clothes who had come in from the night and was Nicanor again, embarrassed with people and seeming to resent their interest even while he needed it.

"I don't know what you want me to tell you; I said I'd come if I could and I'm here. But I can't stay long, I mustn't spend the night here and I must be out of the city by midnight."

"Where then, Nicanor?" asked Hylas.

"Macherus, where else? It's where I've been these last months."

"What's it like?" asked Philo. "How you expected?"

"How did I know what to expect? There are no Romans and that's enough. But I only just got there in time, there's been a lot to learn, and Titus is back, it won't be long now. That's why we're out after supplies. We shall be under siege again before summer, but then we'll show them a thing or two they didn't learn in Galilee. Eleazer will show them."

"Who's Eleazer?"

"My captain."

It was someone different talking, full of hero-worship for his new leader, not the Nicanor they had known. Philo suddenly thought of Conan; Nicanor had asked for him but made no comment when he was told where he was. Perhaps he would come south now; his basic training must be almost over and Philo knew from his own work that there were large troop movements under way.

Hylas got up and said a quiet good night; Philo caught his brother's eye and went out too, leaving Nicanor with Lucia. It was an hour later when the curtain moved again and Philo was still waiting wrapped in his cloak by the fig tree. He got up and hugged Nicanor for the first and last time. There was nothing to say, for they both knew what was happening. Philo closed the gate behind his brother and stood for a long time in the dark before he could face even the tactful silence of Hylas.

XII

A VISION OF JERUSALEM

NICANOR HAD been right, Vespasian was Emperor in Rome now and within days, his son, Titus, reopened the campaign. Philadelphia and the lands of the ten cities were a backwater, and Marius Gallienus fretted as every messenger brought news of troop mobilizations, and it seemed that he would be stuck forever in a forgotten depot. He was fit enough after a winter of exercise and massage at the baths, but it seemed that the generals had forgotten him.

"Here's something that will interest you," he said to Philo one day, flipping a dispatch across to him. "Our friend Sosthenes is on the march. The main muster of auxiliaries will be at Caesarea—not Caesarea Philippi, the other one on the coast—but I wouldn't be surprised if some of his mounted troops come this way. Sosthenes will want to pick up what mounts he can from the Arabians. It's a pity your brother had to go into a foot company. How long has it been now?"

"Only three months. He sent a message once; he knows the caravan leaders who come down from the north."

"I think he'll do well. He could be an officer by the end of the war if he keeps his head on his shoulders."

Philo smiled politely and got on with his work. Hoping to see Conan was not a sensible way to spend time. Every day now the future became more uncertain. During the last months he had settled into a kind of routine that after the horrible winter before had given him time to draw breath, to feel the weight of responsibility grow easier to bear; after all he was fifteen now. Yet any one of the dispatches which passed across the tribune's desk could end his security. When the Romans moved his job would be gone and the house would be empty and tenantless; and they would have gone because of a war in which his two brothers would be fighting on different sides.

Sosthenes' men did come back to Philadelphia; two of his companies had been locally raised and the captain was always hungry for new recruits. Nothing was as effective for that as groups of well-fed, well-dressed troopers off duty swaggering around the market-place, particularly when they had not seen enough real fighting to have frightening tales to tell. Philo watched their arrival without hope. Conan was in the second foot company and they had marched directly to Caesarea.

Then one evening he found Lucia in the twilight, waiting for him in the main courtyard when he left his work in the evening.

"What is it? You're not ill?"

"No, it's Hylas. I don't know what's the matter. He hasn't been out of his room since morning, and when I went in to ask him if he was all right there was something about the way he was lying that made me afraid to speak."

"I'll go and see."

Now he thought about it, Hylas had looked strange for some days, but he had been too preoccupied with his own problems to take much notice. Hylas had slowly grown stronger in body as the days passed; he had made a friend of Gorion and was able to walk with him as far as his house to meet with other men about whom Philo asked no questions. There had proved to be enough copying work in the city to give him the small income he needed, he had seemed serene enough now for a long time. And yet what could it have been except a waiting kind of serenity? From the time when Hylas regained his memory he had believed he had been sent to Philadelphia for some purpose by his unlikely God; what if that God had now given him further instructions? He was like Marius Gallienus really, a man waiting for orders. But not now, thought Philo, not when everyone else is going too.

He pushed back the curtain and went into the little room. Hylas had not lit the lamp and he could see very little until he found it on the table and took it out to light from the cooking fire. Only then could he see Hylas lying on his bed curled over towards the wall, and the parcel of work that Philo had collected for him the day before unopened on the table.

Hylas stirred when Philo's shadow moved across the wall, and turned on to his back. He looked very tired, the way he had at the beginning of his recovery.

"No, I'm not ill," he said, with the ghost of a smile. "No need to look at me like that."

"I'm sorry."

"Philo, it's I who am sorry, I meant to be up and washed by the time you came back. I've been—I don't know how to put it—on a long journey today, and it's made me very tired, but there's no need to weary you with an account of it. I'm all right now, I think, and you have your own problems."

"But I want to know." Philo sat down on his bed, feeling

hurt and shut out. Suddenly he understood how much Hylas had not told him during all these months when they had lived so closely together. Of course this was not the life Hylas had been made for; it was like seeing a fine racehorse quietly eating hay in its loose box and thinking that was all there was to know about it.

"You're going away," he said, and it was not a question.

"Perhaps, that's part of it, but not all, and I'm not going yet."

The relief was so tremendous that for a moment Philo could not imagine what other problems Hylas could have; then he saw that might be just it, still having to wait. And all that time, nearly a year, the unknown friend Camillus had been believing him dead.

"I think I said something to you once, back in the early days when I was still quite ill, about what it cost to be a hero. Do you remember?" asked Hylas.

"Yes, it was when you told us about . . . that night. But you had fever then."

"I still knew what I was talking about! Then I mainly meant the physical pain of going on living when you've been very badly hurt, and I suppose I saw ahead how it was going to be, going on from month to month partly crippled. I've never been a great athlete like your tribune, but I used not to be like this." He put up a hand to his eyes.

"I know it's been slow, but you are getting better."

"Yes, I know that, and I can see for myself that the scars are fading. People don't turn round in the street after me any more. No, today I've been fighting a different kind of battle. I don't ever seem to be able to make things easy for myself; all this time I've been waiting for orders."

Philo made a sound.

"Yes, you saw it, didn't you? Now it's not exactly that they've already come, but I know it won't be long, and when I have to prepare to go I'm frightened. It's been too quiet here, too comfortable, doing work I could do easily, learning Aramaic, being with people who loved me. I have had to learn again that for the moment I'm not free to settle in one place."

"Oh Hylas, why not? That's cruel, if that's what your God wants for you. You said we loved you and we do."

"Think, Philo, I'm only like Conan and Nico, who are both under orders too. It's nothing strange, I'm lucky that I could choose whom I would serve; Conan couldn't. No, that wasn't what hurt so badly. But I think I've spent most of the day in a sort of dream. I was thinking about the future and I was given the power to draw aside one corner of the curtain that hides it from us, and what I saw frightened me. I think I saw Jerusalem as my Christos must have seen it so often, and known what was coming to it. It was as if there was one of those great red sunsets behind it, the sort that come after a sandstorm, and then I saw that the red came from fire and blood, the holy temple was burning, every roof in the city was on fire and the very ground was soaked in blood. There are so many people there, thousands and thousands, driven in by war and fear. Already so many have died that the streets have been choked with bodies, but there are many more who have lived through this already and must still die themselves when the end comes."

"Your God loves Jerusalem, won't he save it from the Romans?"

"If that was his way he would have done it generations ago. I remember once seeing a small child burn himself at a stove. The glow was pretty and he kept putting his hand too near. His father was watching, twice he told him to stop before he hurt himself, once he pulled him away and smacked him, the child still came back. Then the coals moved and the child burnt his hand; he ran out of the room hurt and screaming. If he had gone to his father the pain could still have been soothed away, but he would not give in even then. The Jews have been like that in that they have preferred their pain to a curbing of their will."

"And Conan will be there," said Philo, wiping his face on the corner of his tunic and drawing away.

"Conan will be where?" asked a voice in the doorway.

Philo spun round. There was no mistaking the voice, but the soldier who stood there was quite magnificent.

"Oh no!" At the very moment when the picture of Jerusalem in flames was still burning behind his eyes, it was almost too much.

"What a welcome! Move over, Philo, that's still partly my bed."

Before Philo could greet his brother, Hylas had come forward to take Conan's hands and be gripped hard in return. Beyond them Lucia stood in the doorway. But for Philo it was still too like the snatched hour when they had said good-bye to Nicanor. Both his brothers had come out of the night to reawaken the fears and loves that had gone with them. Conan would go as Nicanor had done and they would not see him again. Their father at least was quietly dead far down beyond the desert gate, at least the dead could no longer hurt in quite this way. He pushed past the others and ran out into the dusk and across to the furthest storeroom.

A little later Conan found him there. Without his helmet and cloak he looked rather more recognizable, but suddenly much more like their father.

"I'm sorry," said Philo, sniffing, when Conan had sat down on a sack across from him. "That was no way to welcome you. You know it's good to see you."

"It's all right, I understood. It hurts, so you wonder if it's worth it. I think it is."

"But what are you doing here anyway? Your company's in Caesarea by now."

"Most of them. I'm part of the commander's escort. I've been in just long enough to wangle that much."

"So it's all right?"

"Mostly, yes. There are bad bits. I've got a friend, though, it would have been worse without him. You'll like Quintus. We're here for several days, so you'll meet him. He's down in the market getting drunk somewhere. I wanted to bring him but he wouldn't this first time, he's decent like that. I wanted to see how you all were. After months and months you never know what you'll find."

"We're all still here."

"So I see. You've done well, Philo, Father would have been pleased."

For a little while they talked about small things; so much had changed that it was hard to know where to start. Then Conan, who had been fiddling with his dagger, looked across at his brother.

"No news of Nicanor?"

"Not since last month, I wrote to you. You got the letter?"

"Yes, so I suppose he's really there, perched in Macherus, watching the western sky over the salt lake for smoke from Jerusalem."

"And that's where you're going?"

"Yes. Don't look like that, I'm not expecting to have to

storm the walls myself, that's what the legions are for. Auxiliaries have the duller jobs. We keep the supply routes open, and guard the prisoners and pick the carcasses clean after the Romans have done the killing."

Some of the fear left him. "You won't be going to Macherus then?"

"Not for the moment, but I think you will."

At first the words did not mean anything. Philo got up and went out into the courtyard and Conan followed him. Then what had been said hit him.

"What do you mean, I will? Don't you mean the depot here, Gallienus and everyone?"

"You too, I think. When I got here tonight, I thought I'd better do things properly, as I was in uniform, and I went to the front gate and reported. I rather hoped I could march in on the tribune and find you at your desk, I was looking forward to seeing your face. But you had already gone and Gallienus was dancing up and down quite full of himself. His movement order is through at last. He's to relieve the officer in charge of the blockade at Macherus, such as it is. I said I was sorry you would be out of a job and he looked amazed and said that of course you would be going with them. Didn't you know? This time, small brother, I can help you pack!"

XIII

SOUTH!

THE LAST OF the horses had gone from the stables and already the living-rooms had been stripped of furniture. Decimus stood in the middle of the courtyard roaring orders, while Fulvius saw personally to the packing of the best mess plate and the Corinthian cups. Philo was still at his desk, but already wearing his travelling cloak and the new heavy sandals that the tribune had given him.

Gallienus swirled in in his helmet and red cloak. “Stop that now, however far you’ve got. I want you down at the barracks to check the mule loads. The man there’s useless. Five minutes to say good-bye to the old lady!”

Philo rolled up the lists he had been checking and stuffed them in his wallet with his writing materials. Suddenly he thought he was going to be sick, but there wasn’t time, no time for anything more. He ran through to the storeyard. Conan was there talking to his friend Quintus. He recognized the look on his brother’s face.

“You’re off? I’ll get everyone.”

It was completely unreal, hugging Hylas and the tearful Lucia.

“Don’t go on so,” said Conan. “He’s not going to fight. He’ll be back before the end of summer. I’ll see him off.”

That was easier, walking back through the archway and down the steps for the last time, with only Conan to think about, not yet realizing that he had seen the others for the last time, as now—in this unlooked-for way—he was at last following his father south on the journey he had dreamed of all his life, beyond the desert gate.

"Hylas told me some of what he told you, before I came," said Conan. "I don't know yet what would be best for Lucia when he goes. Perhaps Uncle Menelaus would take her. I've got a few more days to work something out, and Hylas won't leave her till she's settled."

"You don't mean he might go before I come back?" That had never occurred to Philo.

"No, I don't think so, but who can tell? You won't be away long, you haven't enlisted and you can come home when you like!"

"I suppose so, I hadn't thought of it like that."

Decimus shouted at him. Conan put an arm round his shoulders and gave him a quick hug. "We'll see each other again. After Jerusalem, I'll see you."

Gallienus rode past the gate on his white horse and Philo followed behind him, his bundle on his back, with the last of the mess servants. When he reached the main barracks there was no time to think about himself; the two centuries who had been stationed there would march out within the hour and Philo found himself for the first time in the middle of the ordered chaos of any group of soldiers about to move. For a moment he was frightened; then Fulvius found him, told him what was wanted and where to go when the first trumpets sounded. He slung his pack into the mess wagon and went off to check the mules.

They left before midday; it was a short two days' march south to Macherus. Riding through the market on the tail of the wagon Philo wondered if he would see Conan, but his brother had much to do if he was to see things settled before he went. It was one of the first warm days. Philo leaned back comfortably against the baggage, feeling the relief that leaving Conan in charge had brought him. He supposed he had been stupid not to have realized that he might be needed when the troops marched south, but he had always expected to be left behind with the problems. He understood now a little of what Conan had felt when he marched north to enlist.

The wagon, with men marching ahead and behind, creaked out of the market and under the steep western slope of the citadel. The heavy sandals made the steady pulse-like beat that they had heard so long ago when the tribune came to Philadelphia. He looked up for the last time to the high line of the walls and the corner of the temple roof that showed from here, and thought that his father must have looked up from the same place each time he went south. Then they were through the gate, first among olive groves climbing the steep slopes of the hills above the road and then out on the high plateau, among cornfields and pasture. The road swung south, leaving the pass down to the river and the great rift valley to the west.

They came to Macherus on the evening of the second day. Since noon a *hamsin* had been blowing and the air was hot and full of sand. Philo had been stiff enough to get out of the wagon and walk part of the way, a fold of his cloak protecting his face; he was very tired and parched dry all over. Late in the afternoon they had turned down the road that led to Macherus, and with a sick fascination he realized this must be where his father had found Hylas. He looked down at the baked, rocky ground with its covering of blown sand and pebbles and tried to think how it had been to lie there the year before in the full sun. He was glad that for once it was veiled.

The pass wound down a long way, crossing from side to side of an ever-deepening gorge, till they came on Macherus suddenly at a turn in the road. There was a hold-up ahead and the wagon was halted so that he sat for some time looking across at the place where Nicanor had chosen to live.

It was not how he had imagined it, an isolated fort, more a small city built on a smooth-sided anvil of rock that rose high above deep gorges in a slope from east to west. On that side the rock rose sheer for hundreds of feet above the pass that wound out through the foothills to the lake beyond. The sun had dipped behind the high, level line of the cliffs on the far side of the lake so that the citadel that crowned the walls of the city was drawn against the sky like a dark fang. Up there a few lights were burning already, and there were more in the town, but all lay very quiet under a menacing sky.

A galloper reined in his horse beside the wagon and called over to Fulvius. "Officers' quarters over to the right, below the white rock."

Fulvius pulled the wagon off the road and made for a line of tents which had already been pitched. There were horse lines further down the slope and, beneath the menace of those dark walls, the shouting of men caring for animals in an unfamiliar place in the dark. The ground was trampled and strewn with rubbish.

Fulvius snorted, "Smell that! You can tell it's an auxiliary camp. Who was in charge here? He must have let his men live like pigs. Gallienus will soon have it set to rights, and the perimeter enlarged, though no one could expect a properly laid-out camp in this broken ground."

“Will anyone want me tonight?” asked Philo, suddenly frightened again by the noise and darkness.

“No, find yourself somewhere to sleep. You could do worse than a corner of the headquarters tent, at least that’ll be fairly clean.”

The long leather tent was already up with its awning facing west across the saddle of land that divided the walled town from the camp. The tribune’s orderly was fixing up the trestle table that held maps or food according to need. Towards the back a small curtained-off area already held Gallienus’s camp bed. Boxes and equipment were piled untidily at the sides. Philo supposed that he was hungry, but he was too tired to search for food; he found a dark corner behind the baggage, curled up in his cloak and lay down.

It was a long time before he slept. The ground was hard and the coming and going went on until late. At first he lay rigid, afraid that one of the servants would move the boxes that sheltered him, but they did not and at last he fell asleep.

They came to Macherus at the beginning of summer. It was a month later that, looking out through the shimmering heat down the valley from under the tent awning, Philo saw the smoke in the sky that Hylas had imagined on the day before he left Philadelphia. The tribune heard him gasp and came out to stand beside him, looking above the heat haze over the distant lake to the west.

“Yes, that must be it, Jerusalem has gone at last. Nothing but a whole city could make the sky look like that. Jupiter Ammon, I’m glad I’m not there now. There’s no glory in a massacre, and in that city it’ll be like scything a corn field.”

Philo found that tears were running down his cheeks for

the city he had never seen. "What's that for?" asked Gallienus. "You aren't a Jew?" Philo gulped hard and wiped his nose. "Of course, your brother's there! Well, perhaps now it's over at last we can close our fist round this place and make an end here too. That's if Titus sends us the men to do it. I can stop supplies getting in in any quantity, but with two hundred men I can't do more."

So it was going to begin in earnest. Philo looked across at Macherus; it was still possible to get into the lower town, where a miserable collection of Syrians, Greeks and refugees lived. He had asked Fulvius why they were there when they knew that sooner or later the citadel would be captured. "Where else can they go?" Fulvius pointed west across the great valley. "Look what they've escaped from; can they go back to Jerusalem?"

It would not be long now; the legions would come and that would be the end of it. Was Nicanor still there? The tribune was not busy, although it was clear that would soon change. On the afternoon after the burning of the city Philo escaped from the tent and went down the track that led through the camp gate and into the town below the citadel.

It was blazing hot, the sun pressed like a weight on his head and the heat was reflected back from the sides of the valley. The men at the Roman guard-post on the road were half asleep. They had no instructions to stop civilians not obviously carrying stores and the men were bored. Philo got through with no more than some rude remarks from the decurion who recognized him.

Between the whitewashed walls of the houses it was cooler, flights of steps and narrow streets snaked upwards, back and forth across the steep slope up to the entrance of the citadel. A few old men sat in the deeper patches of shadow, behind a high window a fretful baby cried, otherwise it was quiet. Philo climbed until he reached a wider open space close beneath the upper walls. He began to wish he had not come. What was he going to do? Call up to the Jewish guards moving above the gate, dark against the intense blue of the sky, and ask if his brother was there and would come out and talk to him? That would only get him an arrow between the shoulders.

Nicanor must be in there somewhere, and he would probably never have the chance to be so near him again, and yet there was nothing he could do about it. He squatted down in a patch of shade to watch in the hope that some better idea might come.

He had been there an hour, the sun had passed behind the top of the citadel and the streets behind had begun to come to life, when from below he heard marching feet. The men on the wall heard them too and could see something; a shout brought an officer to peer down and call an order over his shoulder. Philo stood up and ran a few paces back down an alley. Now he wanted to get away without being seen, but in the unfamiliar maze of streets he knew he would soon lose himself.

The marching squad stopped. It was only an armed patrol, but he recognized the tall plume of Gallienus's helmet and two of the other officers, come to spy out the land. They kept well back in the cover of the buildings while the guard fanned out, taking what shelter they could. A man Philo knew, a big red-haired regular, almost fell over him, coming up from behind to guard the alley.

"What are you doing here? Hop it, the tribune'll slaughter you if he finds you up here sight-seeing!"

Philo knew he was right, grinned sheepishly and had turned to go when there was a sudden unfamiliar sound, very close, a whoosh and a thud; a heavy weight hit him between the shoulders and slid down his side to the ground.

Philo jumped clear and turned. It was the soldier lying on his side, his legs kicking while the shaft of an arrow stuck out of his back at a sharp angle. Philo saw the froth of blood on his lips, knew there was nothing he could do and started running. From behind there were shouts, a scream, heavy footfalls and the grinding of a great gate. His feet found a way down the hill, through narrow streets suddenly empty again as doors slammed and the few thin children were snatched up and pulled to safety.

He was nearly out in the open before he stopped to get his breath. The sound of fighting still came from up near the citadel but it did not seem to be spreading. Trumpets sounded across the slope in the camp and reinforcements clattered past. Waiting his chance to get back he realized it was not a general attack, only a Jewish commander taking the opportunity to make trouble. Romans began to come back down the road, two supporting a wounded man, another carried on a hurdle, then a more ordered tramping as if Gallienus had withdrawn most of his men in some sort of order.

Philo made a dash for it, dodging through the guard-post and up between the barrack tents. He got there first but not by much, and before he had caught his breath the tribune and two centurions came in after him. Gallienus gave the last of a string of orders over his shoulder, switched to a comprehensive list of oaths without drawing breath and threw his helmet at his servant. He stood there, big, hot and furiously angry, his cloak slashed by a sword cut and blood spattered on one leg, rubbing a grazed elbow.

Then he turned on Philo. "Don't just stand there!"

Philo sat down at his table, shaking, but before he could pick up his stylus a great hand plucked him off his stool again and turned him towards the light.

"What's that on your tunic?" It was the back he was looking at; Philo did not know. He wriggled his shoulders and it felt stiff, it must be blood from the dying soldier; he began to feel sick.

"You're hurt!"

"No, sir, it isn't mine."

Gallienus caught hold of one shoulder of the tunic and tore it away. Philo's back was unmarked. "You were up there in the city! Why? Who sent you?"

He spun him round and shook the boy so that he could hardly speak.

"No one, I only went to look."

Surprisingly the tribune believed him. "Understand, you do not leave this camp again without permission!" He flung the boy away so that he caught hold of one of the tent poles to prevent himself from falling against the map table. Then as he hung there he felt the first blow. Gallienus had picked up the nearest weapon which came to hand, his ceremonial cane. It could have been a riding whip, but this was bad enough.

Philo had never been beaten like that before, by a strong and angry man. The pain was worse than anything he had ever imagined, as if all his ribs were breaking. Still clinging to the pole he slid to his knees. Above his own sobbing breath and the roaring in his head he heard other voices, shouting outside. Someone said loudly, "Despatches, sir." The blows stopped.

He knelt there, too dazed to move, till another hand caught him by the arm and pulled him through to the rear of the tent and out of the side entrance the servants used. It was Fulvius. He dropped the boy in a heap while he pulled the flap to behind him.

"You little fool! Couldn't you see he'd turn on the first person to get in his way? If Gallienus gets caught in an ambush someone else is going to suffer for it. Let's have a look. Hm, not too bad, lucky he was interrupted, it's mainly bruising. Have you got another tunic?

But Philo was beyond answering. He crouched in the shadow of the tent while Fulvius did what he could for his back and found him a whole tunic.

"Now, keep out of sight for as long as you can, but he may shout for you and then you'll have to go. Of course you can, you'll feel better in an hour. Come round and lie on my bed." He helped Philo to his feet. "At least you didn't yell!"

Did Hylas yell, thought Philo, as he eased himself down on to Fulvius's palliasse. And Gallienus had only been cross, he hadn't really been trying to hurt him. Only then, when his face was safely hidden, could he let himself cry, and it was as much for the brother he would never see again now as for his own pain.

XIV

ELEAZER

THEY COULD SEE them coming when they were far down the plain, the cohorts of the tenth legion, Gallienus's own, winding up the steep pass like an armed snake with the heavy wagons of their siege train. The Jews on the walls of the citadel could see them too and from the camp their shouting could be faintly heard and their tiny figures were black against the evening sky.

"We'll see what Eleazer makes of that lot!" said the tribune, with satisfaction. It seemed a long time since the first sortie. Summer was over and they had got to know their enemies rather better. Particularly the Eleazer of whom Nicanor had spoken back at home in Philadelphia, who had led all the raids into the town.

But Philo had not seen him, he had not left the camp. In a few days his bruises had faded and the tribune had completely forgotten the incident, but Philo had not. Something had changed in him that day, he did not know what. There was nothing he could do about it for the moment, for he could not leave the siege yet any more than an enlisted soldier. Whatever the end was he would see it now and the thought of it never left him; he was beginning to understand the hate in Nicanor's heart.

By the time it was dark the small camp had turned into a large and noisy city of tents and there was a new officer in command, Lucillus Bassus, legate of Judaea. A larger staff tent had been pitched further down the slope and Philo felt strange, looking at camp-fires and smelling the smoke and stink of a whole legion. Conan found him easily.

"I didn't know Sosthenes' Foot were here yet," said Philo, hugging the tall strange soldier who had come in from the dark. Fulvius heard voices, came through to look and then left them together.

"You don't know everything!"

They looked at each other. There was too much between them to be covered easily by words, the death of a city and its people, and the ache, like a wound that throbs on and on, of Nicanor across the valley in the fortress like a fang against the sky.

"You haven't seen him?" asked Conan.

"No, after the first sortie I haven't been allowed to leave the camp. I did try but it didn't work and he beat me."

Conan made a move as if to touch his brother and then let his hand fall. His eyes were very tired, Philo noticed, sunk deeper now as his father's had been after many days in the searing light of the desert. But it had been something else which had changed Conan.

"Nicanor made his own choice," he said. "He doesn't have to be in Macherus. I suppose we don't have to be here either, except once I'd enlisted I didn't have any say in where I was sent. First Jerusalem and then here."

"Was it as bad as everyone said?"

Conan put out a hand again almost as if to ward off the question. "If I knew how to make you see it in your mind I wouldn't, and we weren't in the worst. You get used to some things but others stick in your mind—how people look when they throw themselves off a blazing wall, and there was a woman who'd . . . no, why tell you?"

"What will happen to Macherus?" asked Philo.

"We shall take it, then there'll be a massacre, bad or not quite as bad depending on how long the siege takes. First we've got to prepare the ground. Bassus wants that dip in the neck of land down to the lower gate filled in so he can get his siege engines up close. From the look of this valley that's going to mean back-breaking work for someone; I shan't get free to see you often."

He got up and walked back to the awning outside the tent, his arm round his brother's shoulders, and they stood looking down over the camp. Conan pointed to a row of camp-fires over to the north in a smaller camp across a shallow ravine. The moon was more than half full and the tents showed up clearly.

"Look, we're over there, but don't try to find me unless it's life or death. Some of Sosthenes' Foot are pretty rough. I know where you are."

A voice from the shadows called his name, and Quintus came into the light of the lamps, a stocky, dark young man. "Don't forget we're on guard duty for the second watch. So you are here, Philo, we wondered. It's better than Jerusalem so far, but not by much."

"There are hot springs in the cliffs on the south side," said Philo. "I hear it's almost like the baths."

"After a few days carting rocks for Bassus we shall need them," said Quintus. "Come on, Con."

Philo stood looking down the hillside towards their tents a long time after the two young men had gone. It was good, for once, with what lay ahead, not to be quite alone.

It was some days before the engineering began in earnest. The land round Macherus was rocky, the cliffs scoured smooth by the sand-laden desert winds, and wagon-loads of stone and gravel had to be brought from higher up the pass. Then the work began and with it more sorties from the citadel. The defenders could see what would happen when the ramp was finished.

Philo watched them from the hillside opposite, the little dark figures swarming down through the opened gate, trumpets sounding down at the bridge, the shouting growing fainter as the guards ran into the town and the fighting was hidden between the high walls of the twisting streets, then the last of the rearguard falling back on the citadel. They were small attacks but irritating, and Bassus the legate fumed at the delay. He had had more than enough of Judaea and wanted to make an end. Soon the men of the tenth legion knew Eleazer as well as Gallienus's men did. He was tall for a Jew, with dark curly hair, exceptionally skilled at the hit-and-run fighting that was all that was left to him for the moment. He knew the town, he and his men could appear and disappear without warning. There must be other ways down from the walls than the main gate, but the Romans never found them. Finally Bassus put a price on his head that would have bought a legionary a farm and sat back to see what that would do.

It was on the seventeenth day of the main siege that Eleazer was careless. The first Philo knew about it was when the shouting spread through the camp. He had stopped watching the fighting now; sometimes prisoners were brought in, and he was one of the interpreters whose job was to be at their questioning. It was a brutal business, young Jews, usually wounded, with death in their eyes but still able to suffer and be afraid. Each time there was the sickening fear that the next man might be Nicanor. After the first he had cried himself to sleep, but as Conan said you got used to most things, in one way at least.

Philo had been working—there was more than enough for him to do now, and it helped to go to bed tired—when a different sort of noise started. It was far away, almost at the bridge at first, then spreading up through the camp. If he had ever been outside an arena where gladiators were fighting he would have known what it was at once. Then Gallienus burst through the tent flap.

"Eleazer, we've got him! Come on, you're wanted."

As he pushed his way down the hill through the crowd of off-duty men come out of their tents to stare and cheer, he told Philo over his shoulder what had happened.

"It was the reward that did it, that and Eleazer getting cocky. The attack just now was fiercer than usual and we lost several men. They were auxiliaries—no, not your brother's lot—and they ran for it. Eleazer thought he had all the time there was. He was in no hurry to get back inside the citadel, it must stink by now. He stood there just like Hector outside Troy, cracking jokes with the guards. They'll be the last he makes. One of our men, an Egyptian, got him from behind and frog-marched him out of arrow-shot before anyone could find his bow string to stop him. They're bringing him down now."

Philo made a turn up the trodden path that led to headquarters.

"No, not that way, the legate wants the men on the walls to see this."

They went down across the half-completed ramp and up through the lower part of the town. Guards were everywhere;

Bassus was not risking a rescue attempt. At the top of the slope but well back from the walls was an open space. Already the headquarters staff were there, and the prisoner had been brought forward. High above, the Jewish helmets on the gate towers moved against the blazing blue of the sky. The prisoner, tightly bound, stood in silence looking up at them. To one side a centurion was supervising a working party who were knocking down part of a wall to leave the gate-posts standing.

"Wait here," said Gallienus. "It looks as if you won't be wanted after all."

Philo looked behind him to see if he could get away, but all the streets leading up the hill were jammed with legionaries, peering and jostling to get a view. He was too far away to see what the legate was saying to the men round him but it seemed that the prisoner was not to be questioned after all, Bassus had some other plan in mind.

The centurion had finished; he signalled to the prisoner's escort and Eleazer was led across. Half-way there he seemed to know what was waiting for him and started to struggle. A kind of wailing sigh went up from the walls as he was stripped and tied to the wooden framework.

Philo knew what would happen now and he could not bear it. He had been with the army long enough to have seen men flogged before, but this would be different, not a punishment but an execution. All he had felt about Rome so long before, all Nicanor had said in Philadelphia, flooded back into his mind as he turned and burrowed wildly into the crowd. Pure hatred of Rome gave him the strength to fight his way down through the mass of sweating, heaving bodies, to be away from the noise of the whip that sounded loud in the silence that now lay above the walls, out of earshot before the first whimpering cries came.

Then he was through the crowd and out near the bridge. He took a few steps up the hill and realized that he couldn't go back; he had run away and the tribune would show no mercy either. If Eleazer was conscious later they might still want him to question the prisoner.

He turned to the left and ran down between the rows of tents to the north ravine where Sosthenes' men were in camp. There were few people about; those who were not in the town were watching as well as they could from higher up the slope. Only bored guards shuffled and yawned, waiting for their replacements.

Philo was lucky, Quintus was on duty. He took one look at the boy's face, and saw this was no time to argue.

"You look like trouble! Conan's over in the city."

"I can't go back. Can't I wait somewhere out of sight?"

"Like that, is it? Oh well, third tent on the left in the second row. There shouldn't be anyone there except a man with a flux and you can tell him who you are."

Philo squatted on Conan's bedding roll in the hot smelly tent and had time to think what he had done; the man lying opposite was noisily asleep, moaning and snoring. What was Eleazer to him? A name his brother had followed, the man more than any other of the defenders who had prolonged the siege, had kept them all here in this scorching valley, and dragged out hope beyond what it could bear. His end had come, up there outside the citadel, before friends and enemies together, a slow humiliating agony, and because of it Philo knew that he too had now crossed the boundary against Rome, that he was now one of the ones who must run. But he was a very small pebble in the landslide this death had started; once he was clear of the camp no one would follow him. Marius Gallienus would rage and have a partial search made if he had time, and that would be that. The only problem was where Philo was to go and how he would get there.

He got up and went to the door of the tent, but it faced the wrong way and he could see nothing. It was not long after noon. How long would Eleazer take to die?

An hour later Quintus was relieved and came to look for him. "I don't know what's going on or what we're going to do with you," he said, gazing at Philo with dismay. "I'll see if I can find your brother."

Philo lay down and looked up at the dirty leather roof of the tent. Flies were buzzing and there was the high whine of a mosquito. The time passed slowly. He did not get up to look out again, even when he heard the sound of men coming back through the camp. This was the only place that offered the smallest hope of safety and he did not want to be seen.

It was late afternoon when Conan pushed aside the doorflap and came into the tent. "Come on, quick, they're coming back. You can't stay here."

Philo followed him out, ducking under guy ropes between the close-pitched lines and up the slope behind the camp, past the stink of the latrines into the shelter of some scrubby bushes. Conan squatted down as far out of the sun as possible and looked wearily at his brother.

"Whatever have you done now?"

"Run away."

"I can see that! Gallienus will have the hide off you, you little idiot. Why?"

Philo didn't answer that. "Is he dead? I saw the beginning and I couldn't watch."

"I see." Conan looked at his brother thoughtfully. "So that was it. No, he's not dead. Oh Jupiter, Bassus is a fiend, but he's clever. Well, he flogged Eleazer, you know that bit. The Jews must know what happens to prisoners, but out there in front of them with his friends looking on made it—not worse—harder to bear, I suppose. They made a fair mess of him and then cut him down and left him lying there, and Bassus ordered a cross to be set up, where there was a good view from the walls. You've never seen a crucifixion? It starts bad and doesn't get any better. To watch someone you know—Bassus knew it would have an effect. When they were ready he had Eleazer hauled up and taken over to have a good look; he'd done his best till then, taken it pretty quietly; I suppose he thought it would be over soon. But it can last for days, the cross. Bassus stood and looked down at him, on the ground bleeding, and said, 'It needn't happen, you can stop it.' I didn't see that bit, I was too far away, but it must have been horrible. Eleazer eased himself up and looked back at the walls and tried to speak. His voice wouldn't carry, so they took him a lot closer and then someone shouted up what he wanted to say."

"What could he say?"

"He told them to surrender."

"Oh no! After all they'd been through?"

"I suppose he only really understood what was happening for the first time when they strung him up to the gate-post. Soldiers never think they may get hurt or captured, only that they'll be killed outright, and they don't mind that to start with. Now he couldn't escape what was coming to him, neither could they, Rome would win in the end and death suddenly wasn't the answer. He no longer wanted to die and only they could save him."

"But they couldn't give in! He was only one man. So many have already died."

Conan said flatly, "Did you see him close? I did once in the fighting. He was handsome, there was something about him. I'm not surprised Nicanor could talk of no one else. Oh yes, they've surrendered. They march out tomorrow, though where to only the Gods know."

"Then it's over, the siege is finished. I can go home, Nicanor can too!" But Philo saw his brother's face.

"Is it really over? Wait till tomorrow. As for Nicanor, he was one of the men who came out to carry Eleazer into the citadel when the talking was over. I saw his face quite close too. It isn't over for him."

XV

THE END OF THE SIEGE

AUTUMN WAS well on now and it was cold that night. Philo had wrapped himself in the cloak his brother had brought him and sat close under the bushes, his arms round his knees. It was very dark. What was left of the moon would not be up till later and the sky was cloudy, though there was light enough below in the camp to see what was going on there. It did not seem that anyone had settled down to sleep; the camp was restless and noisy. The men knew they would soon be on the move, back north to winter quarters, comfortable barracks, light duties; some of them were already drunk and there was a fight going on out of sight, round a bend in the cliff.

Conan had brought him food, and a little money; he was on duty now and Philo might not see him again.

"Get away east up the valley at first light," had been his advice. "Don't try it in the dark, you'll be picked up by a patrol, and they don't bother to ask questions these days. Tomorrow the camp will start to break up and there'll be company on the road. You should manage." Conan had looked at him hard then, in the fading light, seeming to try to remember how it had felt months ago when he had first seen a man tortured and learnt how to stay in line and shut the hurt out of the part of your mind that was screaming too, because there was nothing else to do, and stay alive oneself.

Philo's head nodded forward and he dozed uncomfortably, but woke with his cramped fingers in knots and one foot asleep. There was a slip of moon low down at the end of the valley now, so it must be close on midnight, and the camp was much quieter. He saw lights first, then came the new noise, down by the bridge, then a horse galloped hard uphill and more lights showed outside Bassus's tent. A trumpet blew in the section of the camp belonging to the second cohort; from the racket and the shouts of the officers they were all being turned out.

Philo stood up and went a little further down the hill. There was fighting down by the bridge, but who was it? The Jews in the fort had surrendered, and the highest walls were dark and quiet. Someone had broken the agreement, if that was what you could call it. Then the roof of a house just inside the lower walls flared up like a huge torch in the night, lighting up a section of the town, and he understood what was happening. It was the refugees, the people in the lower town, caught like corn between the millstones. The Romans had made no treaty with them and someone had understood what might happen when the Jews were allowed to march out under their safe conduct. The legion was cross and irritable with the siege, and now there would be no glory about the taking of Macherus, no decorations awarded for storming the walls, and no plunder. The citizens were trying to escape before the soldiers' wrath fell on them.

They had only brought it down sooner. Philo watched, almost detached, too far to hear more than a confused roaring, as the fires spread and by their light the men of the second cohort picked off those of the townspeople who tried to escape, like rabbits trapped in the last of the corn. In the dark and smoke the officers did not even try to control their men.

Philo went back to the bushes and curled up again with the cloak over his head to try to shut out the flare in the sky. He wondered where Eleazer was now, if he knew what the price of his life had been for people who had never defied Rome. Had it been worth his humbling before both Jews and Romans, and what did his friends think—did they regret their bargain? And he remembered for the first time in the last hours Hylas, who had kept faith, abandoned his own life completely and received it back in a way he could never have expected. Suddenly he wanted to be with Hylas more than anything else in the world. No one else could sort and smooth and help him arrange the turmoil in his heart and mind with the care of a mother with a sick child. Dawn was still four hours away.

Conan, standing by the road that led down the pass to the west in the early morning light, hoped that his younger brother was well clear by now. There were fewer Jews than he had expected, six or seven hundred, and they had occupied a whole legion for almost a month. Perhaps they looked fewer because they were not marching out as soldiers; there were too many wounded who needed helping and Bassus would allow them no wagons. It was as if he did not want them to get too long a start.

The silent, ragged men passed, mostly bearded, some grey-headed, and few without a bandage somewhere. The heavy, hopeless set of their faces was something he had never seen before, not on so many men together, not at Jerusalem. But then he had not seen so many who had escaped from the siege of Jerusalem alive.

Even though he had seen Nicanor the evening before he wondered if he would recognize him again. But he was there, one of the last, helping to carry a stretcher out through the fire-blackened gate, down a road still littered with the debris of the night's fighting; the last of the bodies had only been rolled out of the way into the deep ditch on the fortress side. He was helping to carry Eleazer. Perhaps they had waited till last because nearly to the end there must have been some who refused to leave the citadel. High above sounded the hunting yells of a century who were searching the walls and barracks, and it seemed as if there was some quarry to chase.

Eleazer lay on his belly, his face hidden in his arms. Nothing showed from under the tightly wrapped cloak with darker patches of blood on it, except the untidy dark hair and one bare arm, the hand clutching at the side of the stretcher. Conan knew that his brother had not seen him the day before; Nicanor could not even have known that he was there at Macherus, he had never asked the name of Conan's company, and yet as Nicanor looked up from the burden he was carrying their eyes met.

One of Nicanor's hands jerked away from the pole and reached towards Conan; the litter lurched and the man on it twisted in pain. Then they were past and Nicanor had his head down, looking where he put his feet. His brother saw him bend down to whisper something in the hurt man's ear and then they were out of sight round the curve of the road and the crowd was beginning to break up.

Conan still stood staring after Nicanor. There had been only one moment when they had looked at each other, he did not even know if his own hand had moved to grasp his brother's, only that they had not touched. What had there been in Nicanor's eyes? Recognition, pain and something else very familiar if only he could think what it was.

Quintus put a hand on his shoulder to turn him away. "That was him?"

"Yes, the young one this side." He turned to look at his friend. "Did I give myself away?"

"No, I don't think so; who would have been looking at you? Even if you did go chalk white!"

"It was something in his eyes—I've got it now, it was the look he used to have when you saw him again for the first time after a row. He didn't know how to put things right, but it was his way of showing he wanted to." His voice dropped and he turned away. "It's so long since I saw him look like that."

"Well, he's alive, and he didn't look as if he'd been hurt. He's strong enough to run if Bassus changes his mind and goes after them."

"You saw him. He won't run away, not while Eleazer is alive, and if he dies I suppose he'll want to revenge him."

His friend led him back up the hill. There did not seem anything else he could say. There was no way for this not to hurt, but like a wound it would heal over. Now Nicanor was so close that Conan could still have run after him, could still have called and heard his voice. On the road north as the nearness went it would be easier.

Then Conan stopped and looked back. "At last he's found someone he really minds about, he never did that in Philadelphia. There was Father, of course, but no one who really reached him. All those years we lived together and played as children and I still didn't know him. I think Eleazer probably did."

Quintus doubled over suddenly, his hands to his stomach.

"Hey, what's this?" asked Conan, looking at his friend properly for the first time that day. He looked grey and pinched.

"Nothing much, only a gripe of some sort. I probably caught it from old Plancus."

"Come on back, here, let me give you a hand. I'll report you sick later."

But before they reached the tent he heard his own named called, Quintus gave him a weak grin and stumbled off towards the latrine and Conan went back to where his decurion was standing with Marius Gallienus. This he had half expected; he snapped to attention, hoping he was reasonably tidy, and fixed his eyes on the left buckle of the tribune's embossed breastplate.

"Is this the man?" the decurion asked.

"Yes, I think so." The tribune's cane was slapping irritably against his thigh. "I imagine you know what I want?"

"No, sir. Is my brother ill, sir?" said Conan, staring straight ahead.

"No, Conan, son of Apollodorus, your brother is not ill, he seems to have run away. Look at me when I speak to you." Conan raised his eyes to the dark and angry face. "He has not, I suppose, come to you?"

"I heard there was a boy in the camp yesterday, but I told Philo never to come here, so I didn't think it could be him." Better to cover himself in case someone except Quintus had seen his brother. At least they could not question his friend in the latrines!

"Where's his tent?" Gallienus barked at the decurion.

The officer led the way, the other men of the company watching in surprise as the tribune inspected the auxiliary quarters, but there was no trace that Philo had even been there; Conan had seen to that.

Gallienus came out hot and very red in the face. "Very well. I suppose he had more sense than to get you into trouble too. But I expect to hear if you have any word of him."

Conan was still standing to attention, his face blank. He could see that the tribune did not believe him, but with the camp about to break up what could he do? The decurion gave him a funny look as he escorted the senior officer out of the lines.

Conan went into the tent, dropped down on his bed-roll and mopped his brow; the sweat had nearly given him away. He was not practised in subterfuge, but there had been nothing else he could do. After a while he realized that Quintus had not come back and went to look for him. Higher up the slope there was a place where the road was clear both ways, down in the valley dark figures moved irregularly a long way off, the last of the Jews. Up to the east there was movement too, patrols going out, and some of the hangers-on who gather at any camp making their way home now there were no more pickings. He wondered how far Philo had got.

Philo had been out of sight of Macherus for the last hour; he had rounded the turn from which he had first seen the citadel months before, without a backward glance, keeping his head down. Then he caught up with a merchant going up the desert road, his wagon almost empty; he had sold the last of his figs and wine and there had been little plunder to buy in the poverty-stricken town. Philo trudged behind in the dust trying to look as if he belonged when a mounted guard clattered past. But Gallienus would not send far for him, he would be busy already with the ritual of striking camp and moving north, the easier way by Jericho and Galilee.

He was not thinking much about anything. It would have been good to see Conan again but he knew it would not have been safe. Philo remembered what his father had told him about his many long marches, when he had asked what one thought about and been surprised to be told nothing. Going uphill took all his energy, trying to keep some sort of rhythm and to ignore his empty stomach and dry mouth. A hundred paces at a time, to the next bend, then the one after. He tried to remember what the road ahead was like, but the last time he had seen it from the back of a wagon and it had looked different.

It was a long way to Philadelphia and he did not know what he would do when he got there, only that he must talk to Hylas.

XVI

THE HOPE BEYOND HOPE

LATE IN THE afternoon of the third day Philo came to the farms at the edge of the cultivated land south of Philadelphia. He had lain for part of the second day among oleander bushes below the desert road thinking he was going to die of thirst, too stiff and weak to move. In the end he had almost crawled back to a place where he was more likely to find help. A kindly trader had stopped and given him water and a lift into Madaba. Lying on a pile of stinking hides in the back of the wagon he had understood a little how Hylas had felt when he was taken the same way. The desert road was not one to travel alone.

Philo was limping from a sore heel as he climbed the last slope to where the road wound into the protecting hills, but on this, the third day of the journey, he was stronger than he had been at the beginning. There had been time to think, for Macherus to grow less vivid in his mind as his feet carried him further away. Then the last bend in the road brought him under the high western wall of the citadel hill to the desert gate and he was almost home. Was this how his father had felt, riding in on a mule with his business done and a welcome awaiting him? Then Philo stopped and went on more slowly. He had been about to take the first turning over the hill. Now some instinct made him pause and think.

He went instead to the market-place. A group of boys he had been at school with were gossiping by a stall. One glanced his way and his eyes travelled across Philo's face with the blankness of unrecognition. He realized how he must look. Philo went to the edge of the fountain and sat down on the rim; after he had drunk he looked down at his face in the water and did not recognize it.

He was filthy, of course, and burnt dark by the sun, his hair a shock-headed mop. His tunic was bleached and tattered where the thorny brush of the desert had torn it and it was much too short. He must have grown a lot and by the look of his legs he was thinner. No wonder that in his own city he had not been recognized. He scooped up a double handful of water to wash his face.

A voice said, "It'll take more than that to make you presentable!"

He looked up into the wrinkled beaming face of old Gorion, who hugged him like an uncle, patted him and held him at arms' length for a proper look.

"I was watching to be certain. You've changed but you're more like your father now. So you are home from the wars?"

"Yes, it's almost over. Over for me anyway."

Gorion, studying him, saw more than Philo realized. "You need a bath!"

The thought of one swum in Philo's mind like a dream of paradise; it had been so long since he had slept under a roof or in a bed, or bathed with warm water; but in the state he was in he had not the courage to go alone. Gorion saw that too.

"Patience! There is a friend of yours not far away, I only left him to speak with you. He will go with you to keep you in countenance and find you a bath slave."

He led Philo away from the centre of the square and over to the arcade where one of Paulinus's shops had been. A man was standing in the shade of an archway looking across at them. Philo checked in his stride as he recognized him, and then Hylas's hands were on his shoulders and he had hidden his face in Hylas's tunic.

"Gorion told me I needed a bath," said Philo, for lack of a better greeting.

"I don't know how you feel but I know how you smell!" Hylas stopped at a stall to buy perfumed oil and pick out an experienced looking slave and then led the way; the public baths were not far off. At the door Philo stood and looked back for Gorion, and then remembered that as a Jew he would not have come in. He turned to Hylas to ask the first of the many questions that must come.

"Later!" said Hylas. "If you don't get scrubbed at once you'll be too tired."

Philo dropped his clothes in a heap on the floor and went through to the hot room. The slave oiled and washed him while Hylas noticed the new height and slimness and the faint scars on his shoulders. It was only when Philo had cooled off and come back with wet hair and wrapped in a large towel, to lie on a marble slab and relax, that he began to talk.

"Did Gorion tell you any of the news?"

"No, he didn't have time. Is Lucia . . . ?"

"Steady!" Hylas pushed Philo back on to the slab. "You haven't been home yet?"

"No, I nearly did and then I came down to the market first. Why?"

"I'm glad. It would probably have scared you to see the house shut up. No, let me tell you, you can ask questions when I've finished. Conan and I discussed what he should do after you went, but we didn't make any changes straight away. Then two months ago your uncle Menelaus died. He didn't leave you anything, but his married daughter has his house now and she sent for Lucia to go and live with her. I think by then she was glad to go and they're good to her. So it seemed better to shut up yours and save money, till we saw who came home from the war and what they wanted."

Philo sat up and started to pull on his tunic. "Conan said she must live with us as long as one of us was left in Philadelphia, and of course we all went. I hadn't realized." Then something else struck him. "But, Hylas, where are you living?"

"With Gorion. Philo, you saw Conan?"

"Yes, three days ago for the last time. He was well then."

It was all back like a picture behind his eyes, the glare of the fires three nights before by the lower gate, the Jewish helmets high on the wall against the sky, the sound of the whip falling outside the citadel. It had to be talked about but not now, not yet.

"I didn't see Nicanor, Conan did. Bassus gave them a safe conduct. I think he will have left the fort, but by now—I don't know."

"I see. That will have to be enough for Lucia, to know that he was seen. She will still hope on even when there is no hope, the way women do."

Philo finished dressing; then, as Hylas had expected, his tiredness came over him all at once and he sat down again on the marble slab, not knowing what to do next.

"Come on, Gorion will be expecting us. You aren't really homeless in Philadelphia, you know!" said Hylas, leading him out.

That was exactly how Philo had been feeling. They walked together up the steep slope of the citadel hill to the little house that Gorion shared with a widowed sister, and there Philo was welcomed and taken in, and ate good food cooked at home for the first time in many months. They had given Hylas a little room up on the flat roof where it was quiet and the light was good for his copying, and another mattress was carried up the stairs, so for the first time for several days Philo knew where he would sleep that night.

After the meal they walked over the hill to the house that had belonged to Uncle Menelaus, to see Lucia. It was a warm dusk with the swallows flying low and the last of the light still glowing in the sky, and as he walked Philo began to see Philadelphia in a new light. Perhaps the day would come when he could reopen the house and live there, but for the moment it was no longer home. The memories that lay in wait in each room were too strong. No, Philadelphia was now somewhere he came home to, not where he lived. How old had his father been when he first took the desert road to learn his trade with an uncle who had gone that way before him? Hardly older than Philo. There was much to learn and even a boy could earn his pay.

He had been walking almost in a dream and he started when Hylas stopped him before the door of his uncle's house. Then there was the real homecoming; Lucia in happy tears, too stiff now to rise from her comfortable seat, but looking well and as settled as one of the household gods in her new home. His cousin was a shy girl whose mother had died some years ago and Lucia's advice with a troublesome baby was clearly proving well worth her keep.

It was long after dark before Hylas took Philo back to their room on the rooftop.

On the next day Philo was up late and it was mid-morning when he found Hylas sitting in the autumn sun outside Gorion's front door. Their eyes met and they went out together without discussion and turned up the hill towards the citadel. A stranger's house was not the right place for what they had to talk about. Up in the small square outside the temple nothing had changed, the leper was still there on the steps and two of the older members of the city council were arguing outside the council chamber as if the last year had never happened. It was quiet and warm. Philo led the way to the place where steps went up to the small bastion on the city wall, facing south and west over the roads that led from Philadelphia, his refuge as a small boy. Without conscious thought his feet took him there again.

Far below a camel train was swaying out on the beginning of its journey, the beasts bubbling and complaining and the camel-boys crying shrilly. Hylas said, "Two months ago, when I could see what would happen here, I wrote to my friend. I thought I had been dead for long enough."

"To Camillus Rufus?"

"Yes, but it may be a long time yet before he gets my letter. I don't know where he is. It may have reached Rome, but I don't expect he's there. Strange to think that the whole width of the Empire may be between us, yet when I see him it will seem as if that distance has never been."

"Your God has spoken to you again then."

"Yes, Philo. Not as dramatically as before, but I think I have understood. My old life has gone as completely as if I had died in the desert, and this last year I have been learning everything again from the beginning like a small child. It was my problem that I learn slowly. I had to discover one can keep nothing back, make no bargains. For most of us what we offer is returned, ours to use almost like a steward. We marry, love our children and work much as we did before. Not all of us, though, and not me. I don't know what it is that lies ahead of me but I know how to begin the journey."

Philo had been hoping he had not understood. The journey that had gone on within his friend's mind had always been one where no one, however much they loved him, could follow, but now he knew that Hylas would leave them soon, the pain was as sharp as a wound.

He looked down at the dusty stones of the wall, with their small lichens and the plants springing from between the crevices. He could not look Hylas in the face. "When will you go?"

"Not quite yet, but before the winter. I was waiting for you to come home, you see."

Philo did not trust himself to comment on that. "Where will you go?"

"I think to Athens first, I have friends there who will advise me. Then to Rome, I can't see further." There was the eager energy in his voice that Philo remembered in his father before a journey. Briefly he grudged Hylas that, and then he remembered what Hylas had come through to reach it, the pain and helplessness and months of weakness and patience. It seemed to him that Hylas followed a hard God.

"I don't know what I'm going to do now," he said flatly. "It's a lot easier to see what I'm not."

"You're not made to be a soldier, nor will you serve

Rome. You could go north and talk to Timon, your father's friend. He would advise you."

"I suppose so. I like him, and I don't want to stay here in Philadelphia. Perhaps he'll have a better idea; he might even give me a job himself. I couldn't stay here; it would be too like things were before, and yet different. But I can't choose what Conan and Nicanor did, I've seen what it's done to them."

"Tell me."

Then Philo told him all that had happened, and the things that had hurt and almost destroyed him sounded small and ridiculous set against the death of a complete nation, the unbearable martyrdom of the Jews. When he came to the tormenting of Eleazer, Hylas held his hand, coaxing him on, knowing that it must be put into words and said aloud or Philo would never be clear of it, like a physician cleaning a dirty wound.

"I don't know what would have been the right thing to do. Every decision that anyone made seemed to lead to terrible things happening. I don't think Eleazer and the Jews in Macherus understood what it would be like, what it would come to in the end, when they took over the citadel. I suppose you can get drunk on more than wine, and men work each other up. The fighting was exciting and there was not too much of it, and no one, none of the soldiers I've talked to, thinks they'll be wounded. They just think they may be killed and then it'll be quick."

"And for Eleazer it wasn't. That I understand very well."

Philo turned then for the first time and looked into his friend's steady dark eyes. Hylas's thought was turned inward.

Philo asked, "What should he have done—Eleazer? I

suppose all he gained for himself was a different death. If Bassus had gone through with the crucifixion the Jews in the citadel would still have died, nothing anyone could have done would have changed that. Because Bassus won't really leave them to go free, he must be hunting them already across the Jordan valley. But perhaps the people in the town wouldn't have been killed."

"It's very hard indeed to die in great pain when you think that your death will have no effect at all. I know, I tried to. Before you reach that far you seem to have been walking towards your death no more than a step at a time, not noticing where you were going, and then it's too late. You can't stop it and there's no way out."

"You would have died if Father hadn't found you, and there wasn't anything you could have told those auxiliaries to stop them. But to be crucified, to see the cross set up and to understand . . . !"

"My God was crucified. Did you know?"

"Then how could he be a God? You've talked as if he still speaks to you. How could he?" What answer could there be to that; was the very light that guided Hylas darkness too?

"To a God is death of a human body the end? He came through seemingly useless and hopeless suffering to . . . it's hard to know how to explain to you."

"Then if Eleazer had died could right have come of it, even though he couldn't see how then, and I still can't?"

"Yes, I think that's what I mean. The Jews might have understood at last for themselves what they were fighting and then they might have surrendered another way, and the people of the town would not have been killed."

"I see. It's not something you can know, you have to

trust. Trust something, your God, I suppose. You did, and now you're here. Whom can I trust?"

"He isn't only my God, you know," said Hylas, smiling. "He belongs to Gorion and more people in Philadelphia than you expect. And my friends in Athens and Rome, and anyone who will turn to him. He is the God of all of us, even if we don't follow him."

"But you aren't going to be here to explain it all to me," said Philo helplessly.

"I'm not going yet, and some things needn't take very long. How long do you need to fall in love?"

Philo put back his head and laughed. "I don't know, I never have, but is it something like that?"

"Very much; better actually. It lasts longer and doesn't shut other people out."

They turned from the wall and climbed back down into the square. It was time to go back.

"I think before I go I can leave you something, enough—if you are really trying to find some purpose in the way your life should go. You've come so far, Philo, from the boy who washed the dirt off me with gritted teeth all those months ago."

Hylas put an arm round Philo's shoulders as they walked down the hill. It was a short walk and yet, with the insight one is sometimes given to recognize things for what they are, Philo knew that he would remember it when many of the painful things of the last months that he had thought never to be free of had faded from his mind. He was clean again, and there was still a little time to draw breath and prepare himself for what lay ahead. Some God, perhaps the still unknown God of Hylas, was merciful.

XVII

NIGHT IN THE DESERT

IT WAS SPRING and the first caravan south after the late rains was seven days out on the road beyond the desert gate, where the high plateau fell away to the great floor of the desert that stretched to the last mountains before Eilat and the sea of Arabia. Philo was stiff and sore, still at odds with the camel he was riding, but not as stiff as he had been five days before. It began to be possible to believe that camel-riding was a skill that could be learned, like riding any other beast.

The caravan leader halted them above the long pass to tighten loads. It would be after dark when they reached the next well and made camp, but you could learn to sleep in the saddle if your mount was no more ill-intentioned than most camels, and the ground was dry so that it could keep its feet. Further back the going had been bad where floods had washed out the road, and Philo had discovered that a fall even from camel height need not break bones. He had been more troubled by the blinding light that seemed to sear into the brain and the blown sand which scoured his face raw; that and the effect of bad water on an untrained stomach.

But the view from the top of the pass was enough to make anyone forget the griping in his belly. Far below, where the plain ran level out into the evening haze, the colours were rose and amber, and there were dark purple shadows from the high outcrops that edged the horizon for as far as he could see, like the bones of some long-dead monster. Closer to, the isolated rocks, their sides cut clean across the strata so that they looked like high-walled castles, seemed to menace the road.

The caravan leader, Timon's steward, was up ahead shouting and getting the beasts on the move again. Philo settled himself into the hard hollows of his saddle and pulled his cloak about him; it was still cold at this height. He felt Conan's letter crackle in the breast of his tunic, the first word that they had received since Macherus; he had been glad that it had come on the day before Hylas went north. Conan was doing well, he was an officer now, he seemed relieved at the turn events had taken in Philadelphia. There was good advice to Philo.

Then in the last paragraph he seemed suddenly to be speaking directly, to have lowered the curtain that now hid his real thoughts. "You will have heard that the legate hunted the men of Macherus until few of them can have escaped."

As he rode down into the shadows of the plain he knew that Nicanor must be long dead. It was useless to hope still as Lucia did, and Conan was trying to tell them that. Even if Nicanor had escaped from Bassus's men where could he have gone? Masada perhaps, and no one could doubt what the end would be there. Apollodorus had died three days' march away from where his son rode now down the desert road, and his second son had already followed him into the darkness beyond. Unless all that Hylas had taught Philo was true and there was a light beyond anything he had ever dreamed of there, at the end. Hylas had been nearer death than any man he knew, and he had a right to speak.

Philo tried to imagine the unknown tribune in Britain receiving after many months Hylas's travel-stained letter. Camillus must be very different from Marius Gallienus. Hylas loved him and to know that such a friend still lived after so long a silence must be a joy as deep as pain. And perhaps they would still meet, across the whole breadth of the Empire. Philo knew he would not see Hylas again himself, it did not help to pretend otherwise. He had wept, after the last dry-eyed farewell, feeling, if he had known it, as Conan did when he saw Nicanor for the last time. But what Hylas had been was still a part of him, something he could lose only if he no longer valued it. The desert road, in Timon's service, was his father's heritage, and had claimed him now. He did not know what lay ahead across the plains and mountains but he was as ready to find out as he had always been.

His camel stumbled and complained, and he prodded her with his foot in the way he had just been taught. A red eye of sun glowed above the dark western cliffs and then dipped into darkness. The plain was like a dim pool below as the swaying line of laden camels wound down towards water and the great silence of the night.

ABOUT THE AUTHOR

MARY RAY has had a passion for ancient history, in her own words, "from the age of six when I started at the deep end with the battle of Marathon, and I have never so far been able to write anything with a modern setting." She writes that since that early time she has never felt any strangeness or distance about what she had learned of the people of Greece and Rome and of earlier civilizations. "I was at home in the period in the way that some people are at home in a place or a country. I started with Roman Britain, because I knew what the places looked like, and for me it is important that the three strands of the actual geographical first-hand knowledge, historical research, and imagination should all be as strong as I can make them." Later, Miss Ray was able to travel extensively to the countries in which her later books were set and in each case makes the reader smell, see and feel what it was like to live in that land.

Born in 1932 in Rugby, England, Mary Ray has had a varied educational and professional life. She attended the College of Arts and Crafts in Birmingham and later trained as a social worker in London and more recently, upon retirement "took a B.A. Hons in Classical Civilisation at the University of Kent and then an M.A. in Church History." She worked in shops, factories, a home for unmarried mothers, in homes for the elderly and finally as a civil servant until her retirement in 1988. Throughout most of this time, in addition to traveling and exercising her creative urge in "making almost anything," she wrote her fourteen books and three plays.

The author's Roman Empire sequence of books, of which *Beyond the Desert Gate* is fourth, is considered an important achievement in the field of children's historical fiction. It vividly captures not only the daily realities of Roman life just after the time of Christ, but also the excitement and tension of Christianity in its early days of secret but astounding growth. Each of the five books takes a different place and set of events, beginning in Corinth (*A Tent for the Sun*), then to Rome (*The Ides of April*), to Athens (*Sword Sleep*) and Palestine (*Beyond the Desert Gate*), and ending in Roman Britain (*Rain from the West*); each book is as different in emotional feel as in the diverse geographical settings. In all of the books the reader is drawn into the interesting, intertwined relationships as much as into the historical period.

Miss Ray writes, "Like everyone who is officially retired I now feel busier than I ever was before. At the moment I live alone with a cat called Phoebe. The children's book market dried up in England, and I am now writing adult science fiction, so far unpublished." So, though she has never written a story with a modern setting, Mary Ray is not one, after all, to look only to the past.